D1091224

THE HOUSE OF BREATHING

THE HOUSE OF BREATHING

STORIES BY GAIL JONES

GEORGE BRAZILLER NEW YORK

I wish to thank Susan Midalia for her intelligent editorial assistance, her consistent encouragement and the various privileges and pleasures of her friendship. Thanks, too, to Ray Coffey for his splendidly incisive editorial expertise.
—Gail Jones

'Modernity' first appeared in
Heroines: Contemporary Australian Women's Writing edited by Dale Spender
(Penguin Books Australia Ltd., 1991).

Originally published in Australia by
Fremantle Arts Centre Press in 1992

First published in the United States of America
by George Braziller, Inc., in 2000

For information please address the publisher:

George Braziller, Inc.
171 Madison Avenue
New York, NY 10016

Library of Congress Cataloging-in-Publication Data:

Jones, Gail, 1955–
The house of breathing : short stories / by Gail Jones.
p. cm.
Includes bibliographical references (p.).
ISBN 0-8076-1455-6 (hc.)
I. Title.

PR9619.3.J6863H68 1999
823—dc21 99-21328
CIP

Designed by John Douglass
Printed and bound in the United States of America

First edition

for Kyra

CONTENTS

THE HOUSE OF BREATHING

Modernity

I

In the history of film there is this poignant tale. A young girl, visiting Moscow from her home in Siberia, goes to the cinema to see her very first movie. She is absolutely terror-stricken. Human beings are visually torn to pieces, the heads thrown one way, the bodies another. Faces loom large or contract to tiny circles. There are severed heads, multiple dismemberments, and horrible discontinuities. The girl flees from the cinema, and as an incidental service to the history of representation writes a letter to her father describing in detail the shocking phenomenon she has witnessed.

The movie showing in that terror-causing Moscow cinema, in, let us say, the bleak winter of 1920, was a comedy.

Imagine this girl. Imagine Siberia.

II

Integrity

In Siberia one knows one's body to be whole because the elements assail it with a totalising force. The air is scintillatingly cold and algebraically precise; there is a mathematical quality to its cutting of angles, its calculable degrees of effect upon the skin, its common-denominative power, its below-zero vital-statistics. In the Siberian cold one feels every extremity, is equated instantaneously to the exactitude of each limb. Even in her favourite bearskin hat, her sealskin coat and her fluffy muff of mink (a gift from the requisite doting Babushka who, in order to buy it, pawned an old grandfather clock from the time of the Tsars), the girl is still rudely recalled to her body. Decked in dead animals she remains feelingly human.

Space

She will push, this girl, through the virgin snow. She will push with her snowboots and her inadequate animal vestments through the all new hectares of still-astonishing white, hectares which, with the sun, will surely bedazzle. She will pass large larch trees hung ornamentally with serrations of ice. Wolf prints sprinkle a pocked track to somewhere. And, looking backwards, she confirms absolutely her own foot-printing pathway.

Space is the lack of conclusion to her horizons. It is the perspectival extensiveness of the trans-Siberian railway, metallically trailing. It is the ample dimensions of snow on snow, so emphatically brilliant that she must squint to discern her journey through every single step of its immaculate empire.

Time

She knows, as we think we all do, time's unamenable incessancy. The clock that used to stand in her grandmother's bedroom ticked in totalitarian and purposive circles. Its hands were definitive, its face as indisputable and blandly commanding as a uniformed apparatchik.

Her grandmother's voice is another aspect of time. Since the death of her mother (a premature extinction in an unromantic snowstorm), this voice is to the girl a regular and reliable instatement of order. Next summer, says Babushka. Last winter, says Babushka. When I was a child of six or seven ... She manages the continuum. There is never any doubting the steady progress to next summer. The larch trees await. The very landscape is bound to perpetual and carefully demarcated mobility. And history itself — by government decree — will later submit to subsections of Five Year Plans.

Setting

Of her home nothing is left to the risks of fiction. It is completely actual and labelled everywhere. The town the girl lives in is called Turukhansk and it sits, in a smug and geographical certainty, at the fork of the Yenisey and Nizhnyaya rivers.

The girl knows this place as she knows her own body; that is to say, with coy particularity. There are parts of the town intimate as her hands, the cobbled alleyway to school, a handsome bowed bridge, the cavities of the market place; specifically a small bakery that, apart from the usual and all-too-familiar black bread, sells light and dainty pastries displayed with memorable panache in its gas-luminous window. There are also unmentionable places and habitations, but she knows these exist as surely as she knows of her own definite but impossibly unregardable heart.

Density

Solid, so solid, is the world of Turukhansk. Once, just once, the girl rode on a speeding troika right out of the town and to the furthest, ice-burdened limits of the world.

There were three snorting horses of massive rotundity — flanks, bellies, the head's bulbous cheeks — and they strove through snow that stirred up in wild eddies and stung incisively. She could feel the muscular energy and rhythm of their gallop; she could see the long heads bobbing and the rim of broad rumps shifting and moving in concert. The breath of the horses was powerfully visible, their odour profound. Bells were atinkle on leather harnesses.

And her father, who seemed himself suddenly newly substantial and corporeal, expanded, upholstered, assuming the impressiveness of horse-flesh, reached over and clasped her in an exhilarated embrace.

Narrative

Do not think that this girl from Siberia is uneducated. Each winter-starless night she follows Cyrillic intricacies stretching in long lines into the mythological soul-land of her Mother Russia. There is the omnipresent bible (Russian in tone), there are the national novels of great solemnity, and there are numerous folktales, all enchanting and instructive. Hers is a country both — contradictorily — filled up with stories and sensationally material. And from her Babushka comes the knowledge of other realms: that she is superintended by the unquiet ghost of her mother, by the never-ending story of family melodramas, by plots of kin.

Sometimes this girl will weep in the dark, not for the banal complications of adolescence, but for the burden of narratives she is compelled to bear, for inner insurgencies clashing with no less force than the Red Armies with the White.

Identity

You will have seen the wooden dolls for which Siberia is famous, dolls which sit, one inside the other, in a series of smaller and smaller otherwise identical versions. These dolls give the girl an image of self: she may be different with, say, Babushka and father, but these selves are all uniform, and neatly composed and contained. She has the conservative's assurance of inner conformity. She knows her self-sameness. Symmetries abound. In the mirror, unquestionably, is her exact adequation.

As she lies awake in the early morning, watching the crystals of snowflakes alight and dispose themselves dawn-lit and lace-wise upon the glass of her window, the girl thinks often of the dolls, one inside the other. She likes to imagine that her absent mother was also, in some way, a kind of replica of herself, that she is constant in image and form even through the passage of generations. By this means she staves off the fracturing power of grief.

Voices

Apart from the management of time and the deployment of story the girl loves the act of voice for its invisible tendernesses.

As Babushka rakes charcoal beneath the samovar she sings in sweet inflections so sonorous and pathetic that her granddaughter, enthralled, feels brimful of emotions. The songs seem to invade her; she swells at their presence. There are neatly rhymed couplets and poetic descriptions of perfect Romances and yearning Love. Language carries within it an irresistible tangibility.

Occasionally, by yellow candlelight, her father takes up a book and reads aloud from the works in translation of his favourite English poet. Once he read of a mad king caught foolishly in a storm and the girl realised, in a moment of vision, that the entire world was Russian, that its rhetorics and its extremity had somehow mysteriously extended to the four corners of the globe. From her father's voice came universality. From the movements of his tongue world-wide concordance.

Bodies

There is a man in Turukhansk so large in circumference that he is reputed to have cut a semi-circle in his mahogany dining table, simply to accommodate his ungainly girth. Babushka loves this story. She is interested in bodies and talks of them continuously. Illnesses. Births. Deaths. Copulations.

The girl touches her own shape with concupiscent affection. She enjoys her baby-fat and her enlargening breasts. She imagines kisses on the bowed bridge and embraces beneath the larch trees. And once every year, when she has a chance to partake of dainty pastries, she recalls the man so large that he must cut out the world in the pattern of his belly.

When the girl leaves to go outside her grandmother offers, customarily, an ancient folk saying: *Rug yourself well or the wind will enter your body and blow away your soul.* This is a disturbing thought. The girl steps into the cold, into its white-blue squalls, hugging her own garments as if they could provide an adhesive to hold her together. In the cold she knows her body better than anywhere else.

Faces

These are indubitable. She studies faces. To see them together you would say that the girl was in love with her father. She gazes up at his face as he reads the latest broadsheet on the trouble in the Stanovoy and Ozhugdzhur mountains. She regards with lover-propinquity his Semitic nose and his brown hooded eyes. She dwells on the crinkles of his balding hair, is captivated by the peaked configuration of his lips. The grandmother, nearby, is of distinctly unSemitic and peasantish visage, but as utterly intimate.

One can kiss these faces. These faces can be clasped between two cradling hands. These faces come with the ponderous and heavy-weighted import of presence.

III

In the especially harsh winter of 1920 our heroine visited for the first time her father's family in Moscow. She descended from the world-famous trans-Siberian railway and fell into the arms of a second, unknown and much wealthier Babushka, a woman who wore about the neck an entire flattened fox, depending sadly nose-downwards.

There was the speed of a slow car, unfathomable chatter, and then the girl realised, incontrovertibly, that she was surrounded by the city. It was a place in which a palpable post-revolutionary unease was contested, again palpably, by a more inveterate aura of historical stolidity. It was a place, that is, in which one might expect dissimilarities and dissimulations.

Faces blurred past. Tall buildings loomed. Red flags, in their hundreds, gestured and stirred.

The visit to the cinema came in the second week. This is what happened. The new grandmother unwisely sent her charge in alone. She equipped her with a handful of roubles and kopeks and left her there at the entrance, a mere babe, as it were, in technological woods.

The girl entered a little late and was perplexed by the darkness. There were straight rows of people — somewhat like those assembled for the pantomime at home — but ahead, inexplicably, was not the space for dramatic action but a rectangle of snowy screen. It stretched across the wall, pure and auspicious. The girl took her modest place among the rows of spectators, of whom she knew not one, and patiently waited. Somewhere to the left a man began slowly playing an inconspicuous piano. Then there was a soft whirring sound behind, like the wind in the eaves, or the wing beat of cabbage-moths, and a long cone of white light shot instantly above her head. This was a bright enlightenment, newfangled, stunning, a distillation of incandescence too shiningly imperious to appear in any way artificial. It might almost have been some kind of Divine Revelation, the trajectory, perhaps, of a passing angel, a signal through space, the pointing finger of God. The girl felt her girl's body tense up intolerably. There was a sensation in her chest of flight and flutter. And then, before another single second had a chance to pass by, there were Russian-letter titles (mysteriously writ), displayed broadly and boldly upon the screen. So that was it. A type of large book. A system of pages. Communal reading.

The piano player pounded a crass fortissimo.

What followed was devastating. The titles gave way to a regime at once human and strikingly inhuman. By some dreadful magic the players appeared to have been robbed of both colour and regularity. Their faces and clothes were crepuscular grey, and their sizes expanded and diminished with awful elasticity. Moreover they moved wholly within the frame of the rectangle; they did not seem to inhabit any ordinary space. It was some condition of suspension within which bodies were dangled upon the screen in a peculiar coalition of living-semblance and deathly, wraith-like abstraction. Thus transfixed these victims were rendered mute; they cavorted in dumbshow, mouthed words ineffectually, produced verbal nothings.

(And rising above the piano was the almost deafening sound of a battering heart-beat.)

It was at the point when the very first close-up occurred, presenting, in the blink of an eye, a gargantuan decapitation, that the girl suddenly comprehended what it was that she saw. It was her mother's death. As the cruel Siberian wind cuts and slices, so too this dissection of the human body. This was how, in her imaginings, she had figured the long-ago maternal dissolution; that a woman, snow-bleached and lacking in the gust-resisting weight of the living, lacking the heaviness of fat men who create the world in their own shape, lacking the cosy enclosure of animal garments, the density of horses, the authority of Babushka, the accessible face, had submitted to execution by the Tundra winds. Bits of her body had exploded into the tempest, disassembled, sundered. Bits of her body had become indivisible from the blurring snow; her inner warmth was ransacked and replaced by cold, her face obliterated, her cry silenced, her soul blown away. In the terrible pelting of the pitiless storm her houseless head was blasted, rendered hollow and windowed as the carcass of a doll. Wracked. Wrecked. Breathtakingly undone.

The girl from Siberia sitting, bolt upright, in the fourth row from the front was completely terror-stricken. There, caught uncannily on the unreal screen, with its distortions of scale and time, its slow dissolves, its clever montage, she had faced in chimerical vision her own perilous vulnerability.

She fled from the cinema, her screams piano-accompanied.

IV

This was a moment of modernity. All that had been solid melted into air. Not electricity or the revolution, not plane travel or radio, but the cinema had inaugurated a new order of perception. The girl of the story was not, as it happened, called Anna Akhmatova or Marina Tsvetaeva, but like the poets she had experienced the metaphysics of fragments. She ran screaming into the winter light of the city of Moscow carrying in her head an unprecedented multiplicity.

Yet when the girl returned home, when she arrived in the arms of her real Babushka — expecting at last to retell the dreadful vision, to collapse, to cry, to blubberingly divulge — it was not cinematic disintegration she described. She did not tell of the deranged and incoherent bodies of the players, nor of how these recalled to her a personal haunting. Instead she dwelled, in concentration, on single detail: there had been a cone of bright light, a white passageway of floating motes, delicate, enchanting, apparently transcendental, which might, after all, have somehow mystically signified the transit of angels.

The Astronomer Tells of Her Love

I

I recall you now with importunate precision. You lay on the bed, languid after love, your body angled to catch the tiger light falling brightly and goldenly from bamboo slats at my window. Remade as animal, ideographed into jungle life, you were suddenly light-lit, embraced by stripes. As you rolled onto your back, the stripes rolled over you; I saw your buttocks disappear, your chest arise, your face orientate. A more careful inspection (bracketing, that is, the new-made animal of such shifting, such amazing, such special integument) showed your face still human. On its illumined side lay a lively eye not quite caught in its net of fine wrinkles, at the temple the beginnings of human grey hair, at the mouth with full lips the human possibility of intimate words.

I bent down above you, almost bridally blushing, and fixed upon your lips an impeccable kiss.

Tell me, you said, tell me about the sun.

The sun, I said, is large and volatile. Its diameter is over one hundred times that of earth, its volume thus something in the order of one and one-third million times. The surface temperature has been estimated at about thirteen million degrees Centigrade. The centre is where nuclear reactions take place, producing the energy that keeps the sun shining.

More, you said, still wetted by my kiss, still light re-defined.

The boundary of the sun, if you can call it that, is known as the photosphere. Bright localised areas are called faculae; then there are sunspots, which appear as dark and sometimes as cavities, and granules which move incessantly over the solar surface. Granular patterns on the surface show us the sun's state of turbulence.

Faculae, you said, mimicking my accent. What a wonderful word. From the Latin, for torch.

We talk, I said, of quiet suns and active suns. Quiet suns are those in which sunspots are minimal; active implies sunspots and flares in great number. Sunspots are my particular interest and area of study.

Mine would be *faculae*, you said somewhat smugly, and turned over again, setting your precious pelt slowly sliding, taking your human face further away.

II

On the beach beside me I saw you bright. In the sunstruck light, reclined and vulnerable, you were more tenderly white-coloured than I had expected you to be. The ghost of your shirt could be traced in pallid areas on the planes of your skin. It was a body unaccustomed to sun exposure, a body still showing, in prissy neat outline, the site of its prior, civilised coverage.

The sun had nevertheless endowered you with sunspots of its own. I noted for the first time the number of your freckles, inconsistencies of colour, granular surfaces. Across the arc of your chest were flung spots by the dozens: and how my fingers longed to properly enumerate! Lower were the curves of soft and kissable skin so hidden as to be almost a lunar blue.

My gaze shilly-shallied with amatory distraction between the day-time and night-time spaces of your body.

Your face was eclipsed by the encirclement of a sun hat and without seeing I knew that it was burnished as brass. Refracted light through straw would generously lacquer; there would be an opulence to the cheeks, a glow at the forehead, a gloss transpicuous to the whole of your handsomely self-enclosed features.

In its aspect of brilliance the beach was almost intolerable. I had come to this country to observe the sun, but felt nothing so much as the sun's observation. The air in Australia had too much light, was too abrupt, too insistent, too filled up with sting and excoriation. Bodies were more definite, shadows were darker, skin almost flinched. Yet I lay there forever, prone in the glare, comfortable with the shape of your resting beside me.

From beneath my straw hat, my own circle of shade, I watched like a spy. Tiny grains of sand lay resting indistinctly in the hairs on your arm. Your chest rose and sank; your skin was tinting pink. An ear had escaped the compass of your hat: I looked into its curlicues and thought with your thoughts of the sound of the sea, how the waves, so close, pushed up and dispersed with a gentle collapse, how the low pitch of wind interpenetrated the water and muffled its splashes, how, with concentration, one could hear one's own breath entering and leaving, in the midst of the sea sounds.

Tell me, you said, tell me more of the sun. What does it send us, we mad dogs and Englishmen, apart from sunburn?

The sun, I said, emits many things. It emits radiation at radio wavelengths. When the sun is very active irregular outbursts of radio noise will occur. Intense radio storms are associated with solar flares. Photons of infra-red, visible light, ultraviolet and radio waves are all ejected. There are also X-rays and cosmic rays leaving the sun at high velocities. We think too there are neutrinos — atomic particles of no mass or electromagnetic properties — which reach us from the sun. These are the by-products of nuclear reactions at the centre of the sun, but are as yet somewhat scientifically elusive. Colleagues in America, in North Dakota, have placed a tank of forty thousand litres of cleaning fluid in a goldmine one and a half kilometres deep in order to capture and calculate neutrinos from the sun.

At this point you laughed. Ah my text-book lover, you whispered under your hat. My crazy professor. My know-it-all scientist.

I did not feel encouraged to explain the experiment. The sound of the waves filled our wordless interval. Your lips, I supposed, bore the hint of a smile.

There is also solar wind. Interplanetary space is not empty, but contains, as well as dust and other meteoric particles, a magnetised plasma originating from the sun. This material streams away radially and at high velocity, and is composed, among other things, of positive ions, principally protons. As the sun rotates the solar plasma sprays outwards, creating a spiral of force lines right throughout the solar system.

I paused for response. Like a dancer, I added, hoping to please. Like a dancer with long skirts, swirling out colour.

You lifted the corner of your eclipsing sun hat and peered superciliously with one sea-green eye.

I zee, you said, in Hollywood German. I zee you are becomink incompetently metaphorical!

You rolled and drew me near and our sun hats collided. I felt a creaturely warmth in the salty pores of your skin. And on your lips the very taste of the sea.

III

Of all my private garments you liked more than any my *chinoiserie*. It was a lapis kimono spattered with chrysanthemums and held at the front by a simple satin tie. When I first wore it you adopted — as only you would — an extravagantly theatrical Chinese accent.

Ah so! The woman astronomer comes clothed in deep space! See the many round suns that populate her blue! See how they orbit and swerve on her hidden entity! See light fly out! See sunspots! See *faculae*!

These are oriental chrysanthemums, I sought to explain. Double blossomed chrysanthemums, a traditional design, and bought, from someone who knows, in the city of Hong Kong.

Ah so! I shall kiss this sun, and this one here (and you kissed the chrysanthemums that lay above my breasts) and I shall slide my slender hand into this star-white gap to destroy all gravity! (And you slipped your hand nimbly through the opening of my garment, finding the fleshly gape, the introductory recess, and I felt it close softly on a nipple, on a breast, and began, at that moment, toppling away towards my bed, falling through a space made instantly accommodating by sweet expectation. I felt hair from your forehead brush lightly against my cheek. I felt my satin give way to your five fingers' bold and astronautical exploration.)

IV

Eventually I managed to show you the sun. A quiet sun had been displaced rather suddenly by an active sun, so I took the small telescope I had owned since childhood and set it up in the garden. I inserted a Huyghens lens — which is the one used by amateurs to withstand the sharp heat of a solar focus — and placed beneath the eyepiece a sheet of white paper pinned onto a frame. By this simple method a projection appeared and I was able to show you the cluster of sunspots I was engaged in studying.

Sunspots, I said, have a particular structure. The core is the umbra; the lighter region beyond the core is known as the penumbra. And you can just see, if you look very carefully, a suggestion of filaments shimmering around the penumbra and radiating outwards.

I watched you bend closer. You studied for some time the disk caught on paper. The light on your neck made it orange and adorable. The hairs on your neck curled up in tight curls.

Where are the *faculae*?, you asked at last.

Here, I said, gently shaking the frame. You only notice faculae when the image moves.

You bent over again and watched as the bright spots, so casually indiscernible, became visible by motion. Pinpricks of radiance, like small perforations, slipped here and there over the surface of the paper.

Ah! you exclaimed, raising your face with its prepossessing smile. Ah!, there they are!

V

My bedroom was an entire, bamboo-screened world. It was quiet, but not still; I liked to imagine the sensation of rippled floatation, as though the whole house was transported and somehow mysteriously sea-borne.

Since your body was sunburned I treated it gently. I poured scented oil into the cups of my hands and with the tips of my fingers spread it with care. The rounds of your shoulders were a painful vermilion. Your nose blazed red, your cheeks blushed bridal. My fingers drew shine over your trembling eyelids.

With the sun too low to present you striped, you were represented human. I traced out your form with the application of shine; I enhanced its morphology, rendered it aromatic, refigured by subtle distribution of light its planes and shadows and skin-sensitive enclaves. Under my lubricated touch you were lustrous and singular, oil-lovely, supine. Chest and abdomen submitted to my caress. I trailed bronze routes with single finger delicacy, then opened my hands for a more generous fondle. At your hips, causing pause, was a triangle of white which showed, perfectly outlined, the template of your bathers. And within the triangle, as though eccentrically framed, lay the bulbs and the bumps of your splendid genitals. With the restraint of an old nurse I dawdled my slow fingers in the chaste area of your chest, and recalled, over your body, the soft tumble of waves you taught me to listen to. I heard the water and the wind, unquiet, implacable; I filled up my room with the sea sounds you had given me, sounds I had never quite heard until, on the beach, your eyes spangled and bright, your intelligence attentive, your ear alert, you said to me: listen!

VI

When we met one day at the new coffee shop I showed the paper

I had written on prominences. You lifted your face from its feed of croissant and pushed back a cup.

Always ready, my teacher, to become illuminated!

Your tone was ambiguous. From your head you doffed an invisible cap (invisibly feathered) and swept it very low in an ironically Elizabethan gesture of deference.

I watched your freckled hands shuffle away at the papers and knew at once that you would not wish to read what I had written. I tried to entice. Prominences, I explained, are the most beautiful and spectacular of solar phenomena. They appear at the edges of the sun as flame-like clouds taking shapes which astronomers classify familiarly, according to earthly analogies. So there are rains, funnels, trees and even hedgerows. But the shapes themselves always evade these classifications: they only approximate what we describe; they are more multiple and inexact. They are also perverse. Prominences give the impression of surging way upwards but are often, in fact, flowing down to the chromosphere. They are brilliant and impulsive; they work both in puffs and gaseous surges.

Your hand had slowly reclaimed the cup. Your eyes were downcast, studying, it seemed, the shallow pool of coffee. A flake of croissant had caught on your chin. As I leant carefully forward to attempt to remove it, offering public tenderness, you leant back rather quickly, startled and furtive.

Must rush, you said, and in an instant were gone.

VII

We ceased meeting in the day and by night you could not bear the revelation of lights. I should have known but did not — in the stupidity of love — that your decision for darkness was bound to be significant.

You said: Your observatory eye, you are greedy, you peer, I am an object of surveillance!

So that night I clasped a lover that was mere silhouette, arrogated and transformed by the dark of the night. When we rolled together I could not have been sure who you actually were:

it was a presence I rolled with, a sort of reversal. I felt your weight upon me, heard the wind of your breath, but was still uncertain.

Together we met in a blind entwining, hopelessly benighted. I ran my fingers over your features for an exact certification, anxiously seeking a message in Braille. I groped and fidgeted, lover-inept.

When our bodies parted I waited for words but they did not seem to come. Then as I began at last to speak you straight away intercepted:

Fucking pedant! Your intellectual arrogance! Positivist! Scientist!

And the darkness pushed between us like a dissevering wedge.

VIII

I remember, now, with importunate precision. On our last night together I wore silver stellar ear-rings and an Indian silk scarf. The fabric of my dress was soft and voluminous. My legs were clothed in stockings; I was beautiful, full. I disrobed in the light while you waited under the covers. You watched my every movement. You watched as I lowered and unfurled, with seductive delay, the black sheen on my legs. As I slid away the fabric. As I stood, ready. About my neck remained the Indian scarf: I had let it remain as an erotic delectation, a gift, a speciality.

You've forgotten the scarf, you said abruptly from the bed.

I fumbled at the knot (still so eager to please!) and in impatience sent the silk scarf flinging away. It rose up in a trembling arc and descended in slow motion, finding the shape of a series of loose, shiny and undulant arabesques. It tilted in the air, back and forth and back and forth, its range of colours, its gleam, its elegance exotic, released in this simple rockabye of declivity.

A prominence! I exclaimed, pleased with the act of recognition.

And you turned your human face, silently and conclusively, away towards the wall.

Other Places

I

The intersecting other place of this recollection is the island of Timor. On maps it appears as a tiny oblong, hanging at the end of the Indonesian archipelago, floating inconspicuously to the north of Australia. It is small but precise, a material place, with a politics, a currency, poor roads, monsoons, mountains, wild deer. There have been books written about it; it is certified, real. One can point on the map with a confident finger and say: here it is, you see, this is where I journeyed.

But as I recollect now — in this most facile of transportations, this space-negating shift, this cartographical defiance, the island begins to quiver and become deliquescent; it melts suddenly away into the sapphire-blue sea, subsides as easily and tremulously as any fiction.

How to substantiate? How to refabricate the unfashionable 'real'?

Let me begin — distrusting as I do the general and sempiternal — with a central spot and a specific time. The spot is the market place in the city of Dili, the capital of East Timor. Nothing about this market is fixed or permanent; there are no stalls or trestles, shelters or plastic signs, such as one sees elsewhere in commercial Asia. Nor is there anything of the pleasures of exchange, the colour of commodities, the lurid ornaments of display, the bustle of buyers. This is a place which is crude and rudimentary; it is a place of poverty.

Vendors leave their villages in the inhospitable dark, walk jungle miles with straw baskets and slings, and come, eventually and in centripetal procession, to a large rectangle of stone foundations, the only remains of a once grand civic building bombed by the Japanese and never reconstructed. In this vacant site, this blank of a building, they assemble in an imperfect geometry of rows, lay their goods on the stones, squat on their haunches, and wait for light.

When sunrise comes there is a second, more casual convergence of pedestrians. Other poor people enter the place of stones, move about slowly between the human rows, gaze down upon bananas, rice and fish, and begin to establish the equations of transaction. Tiny silver coins of minute denominations preciously travel from palm to palm. There is a certain polite haggling over paltry sums governed by the scrupulous justice of scarcity. Then finally the coins are deposited in laps, in concaves of fabric sumptuously patterned over by triangles, spheres, zigzags and diamonds, intermingled with hibiscus, oleander and plume shaped leaves.

The fabrics these people wear invert the substance of their lives; they carry in representation the proclivities of decoration and embellishment they do not otherwise enjoy. The fabrics are dirty and faded, but this does not at all distract from their quality of anomaly.

As the sun moves higher the vendors will place shallow baskets on their heads to serve as hats. Men stand up from time to time to air their hot genitals by flapping the splendid cloth of their lap-making sarongs.

Women employ fans at beautiful, bronze, emaciated faces — faces a Eurocentric artist might wish to construe in the Exotic Island genre, might render, in consequence, more fleshly and more erotic. But the women at this moment evade the sublime. Their thinness is unpainterly, their poses unconventional; moreover, like the men they chew the oblivion-giving betel nut. Their open mouths appear as cavernous pools of blood; their lips are red-ringed. Jets of scarlet spittle are expertly ejected in long narrow arcs. The betel nut chewing is culturally enclosing; in this way the market women remain narcotic and aloof.

The heat becomes visible in a series of verticals and begins at this stage to corrupt the produce on display: mounds of carmine chillies shrivel untidily inwards; fish begin to stink and turn at the edges; bananas gain spots and exaggerate their curves. By noon most of the sunstruck food is removed. The disappointed people in their anomalous fabrics disassemble the rows and walk away into the sunlight, by now overhead and incandescently severe.

The time of this market is the month of December in 1974. At this world-historical juncture East Timor is ruled over by the remote but not disinterested nation of Portugal.

In the 1520s Portuguese merchants usurped the island, hoping for spices, slaves, minerals, sandalwood; longing, perhaps for the piratical exercise of illicit lusts, the adventure of governance, the amenities of power, the excesses of the imperial. On the Belunese and Atoni, the main indigenous clans, they imposed ineffectually a language and a religion; more effectually they wrought a system of economic deprivation.

Apart from a few ostentatious stone buildings, a church here and there, a makeshift airport, there is little physical evidence of over four hundred years of colonial rule. The people still live in their ancient thatched huts (which come in rectangles, ovals and attractive beehives), still farm in a laborious and primitive fashion (the Asiatic mode-of-production intact, with no gifts of machinery from the mechanised West), still suffer the misery of decimating famines (with the saying 'hunger as usual' as their most famous slogan) and still honour the complex, devoluted authority of tribal chiefs, local allegiances, and matrilinearity (despite the Western exercise of larger and apparently more salient powers).

When, in the august year of 1904, the Luso-Hollandesa treaty finally settled the vexed issue of Dutch contestation of Timor — by granting the West to Holland and the East to Portugal — the people of the island did not appear to celebrate. Maps were redrawn in lavish offices by uniformed men, but life nearer the equator continued unmapped. Rebellions arose and were efficiently crushed; certain uniformed men gained swift promotion. The Imperial mode, with all its cannibal appetites, was, in the language of the smiling victors, 'firmly reconsolidated'.

This tiny half-island is about to be granted independence and nationhood. In the month of October voices in Lisbon announced the future: East Timor would be liberated in 1976. Thus around the stone market, burdened by boredom and watching the leaving women with lazy appraisal, move conscripted soldiers from a regime made recently more redundant, more vicarious and more risible than usual.

The soldiers wait out their thankless historical allocation, their — let us say — devious misplacement. They slump with their rifles in the immoderate heat, or drive in failing jeeps over treacherous roads. At night they will gather to share subsidised wine which bears on its labels the names of their home towns and then, as if in this far colony mere names were enough, they will drink and drink until the name enjoins fluidly with the cascade of alcohol so that they are flushed nostalgically, rushed away, sent buoyantly backwards on bargain basement currents to the places of reference. Noise will ensue, prostitutes will be found, and the men will eventually return, sodden and saddened, by way of all flesh.

The soldiers are already anticipating the wine; you can see it in the focusless vacancy of gaze that follows only vaguely the women's dispersal.

II

Into this scene and this time steps an inexperienced young traveller in search of lunch. She steps over hot stones which bloom, like a garish carpet of disordered poppies, with a thousand spat blossoms of dried betel juice. Most of the food is already removed; she settles for a hand of pink-coloured bananas from a man slow in leaving.

A group of soldiers nearby start to whistle and raise their voices, noting, apparently, the familiar vulnerability of the single female. She becomes self-conscious and is suddenly tentative. She retreats uneasily, lassoed by looks and knowing she has supplied some extra code of exploitation in the ease of her capture.

Over to the left — past the official white-washed buildings and the modest Hotel Turisto, past a cluster of shabby Chinese owned shops, from which men invite, with blackmarket obsequiousness, the exchange of Escudos for dollars, past a barracks storehouse, a tawdry bar, a pearly monument of the Virgin hovering unnuminous at a street corner — a commotion occurs to intercept our little drama. A speeding truck, upon which chanting men are crowded, swings into view.

In the traveller's sunglasses the truck is reduplicated; and its miniatures enlarge as it speeds towards her. She forgets the soldiers and the soldiers forget her. They have lifted their rifles. The young woman leaps back against a stucco wall pockmarked by bullet holes from the last world war and smells in the same instant the scent of squashed banana.

The men on the truck, some in Western dress, chant 'FRETLIN, FRETLIN, FRETLIN'.

Their arms are upraised in a revolutionary salute. They are weaponless and smiling. The truck begins blurring past, speed-transfigured, but then it skids unexpectedly to a jerking stop. The soldiers tense up, hoping, trigger-happy, for trouble-to-write-home-about, for significant danger, perhaps a glimpse of atrocity, but to their disappointment are hailed in the friendliest of fashions by a civilian white man who has climbed down from the back of the vehicle. He is apparently enjoying his anti-climactic arrival; he laughs with the others before he signals with a wave for the driver to move on. The chants resume their noisy barrage of fricatives: 'FRETLIN, FRETLIN, FRETLIN', and the miniatures diminish even faster than they arrived, and no less animate.

Our traveller is stuck in a tight clasp of time: the heat is arresting, the sunshine vertiginous. She will later reprimand herself for so public a fear, but now she looks up and her sunglasses receive, in both smooth screens, the approaching white man.

He ambles towards her, halts within inches, smiles politely, and bends to his knees. Then without yet speaking a single word of hallo, he removes a handkerchief from his pocket and sets about wiping a smear of banana from the cloth of her skirt. The traveller keenly watches the top of his head; there is a definite circle of premature baldness which, with its simple ordinariness and rather more complex invitation of caress, unfastens the clasp and replaces the instability of the moment. There is also the cleansing gesture which, mediaevally supplicant, modest, deftly intimate, compels above all her act of attention.

III

Shall I lapse sentimental? Connive with the expectation of traveller's tales confessions? Lust and indiscretion in foreign lands? The suppliant embrace of a sultry stranger beneath silhouetted palms and a crescent moon?

No commodious clichés embrace these memories: I cast about, circumlocutory, for forms of expression, and find myself recentred on the candour of the specific, on the fallible face, on the miserable inexactitude of what one believes to have been actual.

I met Patrick Donelly when he bent to wipe banana from the cloth of my skirt. At that time he was working as a doctor in the Dili hospital, the only foreign volunteer, I was later to discover, among a population of medicos conscripted from Portugal. I looked down upon his head, and thought his simple action a signifier of romance: I thought him gallant and prepossessing, assumed, by his confidence, a certain dynamics of physical attraction.

As it happened this was mistaken: Patrick had stopped because he thought me a visiting Australian journalist (rumoured to be arriving any day that week) and wished to enlist aid in publicising the country's shortage of food and medical supplies. His motive was political, his disappointment evident, and I, in response, felt awkwardly apologetic. When we later lunched together — over tiny buffalo steaks and large mugs of red wine — we reconciled our mis-meeting through slight inebriation and the easy cameraderie of dislocated persons.

Dr Patrick Donelly was garrulous and comic, but one of those men whom one knows must carry an undisclosed gravity tucked somewhere within. I recall that even from the beginning I watched his face with a lover's interest, noticed the flaws of his skin, an uneven shave, a slight asymmetry of features. With the elapse of time this face is now posthumous, yet I remember it with all the precision of originary presence, as though Patrick is still alive somewhere to claim and confirm his own memory-dispersed image.

And this — let me be candid — is the burden of other places: that they are contiguous in recollection with one's lost affections, that no matter-of-fact, sensible, or contrivedly objective description, nor, I might add, no sentimental style, no encircling banality, manages quite to dispel the aspect of personalised elegy.

So there is Patrick Donelly with his mug of cheap wine, sitting beneath a neat dome of pink and mauve oleander, sitting in the shade of his modest thatched hut — at once singular, humorous, erratically handsome, unaware of the fast approaching cruelties of history, and thus assuming, as we all do, a disposition and an aura of fortunate permanence.

IV

Into the highlands, rude as conquistadors. The car imperious, the subjugation of space, the tourist-whizz of lives caught snapshot emblematic. Voluptuous green. Animals in flight. The thrill of collapsing and transitory images.

The ostensible reason for our trip was vaccination. We loaded an army jeep with medical paraphernalia, and drove off in the company of one Afonso Vieira, a soldier of high rank whom Patrick had greeted, to my jealous dismay, with a prolonged and passionate kiss upon the lips.

We three sped into the hills, left the coastal plain and rose into the emerald and abundant forest, into dominions and repetitions of tidy padi field, past high hills prodigious with Arabica coffee, through scatterings of village life (chickens leaping directionless in a flap of feathers, children racing alongside, workers pausing to register the shape of our invasion), along serpentine roads only speculatively in existence.

Afonso, not I, was the lover of Patrick; in our several weeks together we noted in each other the same kind of longing. There was the same conjunction of attention, forms of copycat behaviour. Our desire enjoined our gazes and led us secretly to a respectful and affectionate collusion. But my rival clearly carried the poise of the chosen: he drove determinatively, smiled, laughed.

In these highlands, said Patrick, there exists a tribe of elusive cleft-palated and red-haired people whom I have never vaccinated. Such seclusion is both admirable and medically inefficacious.

In these highlands, said Patrick, fifty per cent of babies die in their first year of life. Yet the mourning is never attenuated or any the less impassioned.

In these highlands, said Patrick, there are whole villages of people who through dietary deficiency develop goitres on their necks. Some carry formations the size of rockmelons, like marine encrustations.

In these highlands, said Patrick, the population is among the most deprived in the world: you will notice some children disturbingly skeletal. Their bones are as fragile as sticks of chalk.

In these highlands, said Patrick, Fretlin forces are gathering.

They are a nationalist group whose philosophy, *mauberismo*, is the liberation of these people, the poorest of the poor.

When Patrick was not talking he sang, in his beautiful bass, the blues of Leadbelly and Robert Johnson. It was a peculiar distraction. We careened round mountains, passing through canopies of dark shadow into oleaginous yellow light, shadow, light, shadow, light, and backwards, windblown, flew negro melancholia. Afonso hummed along; I played the records in parallel in my head, and glimpsed through the window disturbingly skeletal children (entirely unmitigated by Patrick's prediction) pivot to our engine sounds, leap up and weakly chase. (Later the goitres would also shock; there were women so deformed that they appeared almost to possess a second head at their necks.)

The place of our arrival, the base from which we worked, was the district governor's house in the southern region of foothills. We camped with our gear on the open verandah, and set off each day on medical excursions. I remember that Patrick and I dressed in the sarongs of the country, both mock-indigenous and also appropriating, as it were, that consolation of decoration in such grim surrounds. Afonso, I must add, retained his military uniform, and thus commanded servility in every village he entered.

Together we became acquainted with the rigamarole of suffering. We performed doctorly deeds in situations of distress. We were utterly insufficient.

At this point my recollections condense and centre. After goitres, hypodermics, and anxious faces (the melodrama of the true, as Patrick called it), after mad buffalo and gentle deer, after cliffs and rivers, after the denudations of labour and the exhaustion of pity, there is a single special night I remarkably retain.

We had retired rather early to our hard straw mats, and entered, for some reason, on a contract of confession. As children on a school camp — lulled by the expedient communality of darkness, intimate by virtue of the treat of proximity — might choose, in the small hours, to offer up long kept secrets, so we each agreed that night honestly to disclose. Firstly we agreed to talk of some other place, to refuse where we were and to transfer elsewhere. We agreed also to speak of something risky and private, something never before revealed, something that, in the morning, we would hold secret inside us.

By a kind of desperate ventriloquism — since their voices elude me, since I have a tongue and a body and they are mute and incorporeal — I now break open our contract and record these confessions.

It was a moonless night. There were poinciana aroused by breeze, spiralling mosquito coils, oppressive heat.

Afonso: When I was a child we lived in Sintra eleven kilometres from the coast. Do you know Portugal? Well Sintra is not far to the north-west of Lisbon. It lies at the foot of very jagged mountains, so that the scenery all around is green and spectacular. There are two famous castles, set apart and aloof, on a single peak, and these castles appear and reappear throughout the town, and especially in the capital, on the faces of postcards. So you say the word 'Sintra' and visitors who have been there will think not of villas and apartments of stucco and tile, ancient pastels and orange roofs crowded too close together, communal washing, in the poor quarters, flapping gaily above the streets; nor of the more private wealthier houses that are walled and secretive, sprouting lush gardens, also pastelly and old; they will think instead of the famous castles. One castle, I should have mentioned, is merely fancy ruins: it is Moorish, eighth century. But the other, the magnificent Castelo da Pena, is exactly as a world famous castle should be, fulfilling, as they say, the requirements of imagination. It is of pale grey stone and is a complex arrangement of towers, cupolas and battlemented walls. It is a fairytale vision; it is solid but fabulous, and it is utterly unconnected to the reality that is Sintra.

Children in the town liked to make up little stories about the Castelo da Pena: we lived, you see, almost directly beneath it; it hovered over our heads like a persistent dream and on cloudy days it appeared suddenly more dreamlike than ever, remote, vague, apparently floating. It was like something transported from the realm of picture books; it didn't look as if it ought to exist there in the mountains, which we knew as ordinary, the territory of our picnics and Sunday outings.

The place I return to when I think of my childhood, when I think of Sintra, is not the famous castles — which, incidentally, I never actually visited — it is my grandmother's room. We lived in a grand villa behind a huge wall so that the house I grew up in was engulfed by shadows. But my grandmother's room was built like an attic: that is to say it projected above the roof and above the wall, so that it was wonderfully sunlit and looked out onto the world. From one window you could actually glimpse the Castelo da Pena: it was as though she possessed her own private picture postcard, enlarged and extra clear, framed upon the wall. It was one of many pictures because my grandmother — Nina, her name was, and that was how I addressed her — Nina was a collector of religious icons; and all around the room, on the same level as the castle, were the faces of saints, madonnas, pathetic looking Jesuses, and blue-winged angels. She was very devout and was never seen without her black lace mantilla, so that you would always think she was dressed up and ready to go to church. When she was inside, inside her own room, she still wore the mantilla, and I used to place my little-boy fingers in the eyelets and loops and flower-holes of the lace as she cradled me in her arms.

Nina's room was special not only for its light — which covered its spaces in a variety of yellows and always distinguished it beautifully from the submarine gloom of the rest of the house — but because of her eccentricity. I was not allowed to enter without bidding good day to each face on the wall and then, for some reason, saluting the castle with a kind of parodic militarism. This done Nina would spread her capacious body on an old chintz lounge that lay beneath the window, and I would run and leap onto her, collapsing with giggles into her pillowy breasts, the drapery of her clothes, her womanly, musty, mysterious scents. Then — and it always happened exactly like this, time and again! — I would position myself against her so that I could pull the end of the mantilla across my eyes and look around the room through its complex fine tracery of black flowers and holes. This simple transformation always enchanted me: what was gold became suddenly shaded and dark stencilled;

what was known became strange and obscurely dimensioned. Overlays, underlays. New configurations. Faces redesigned. As I fiddled with the lace Nina would start to chatter away in a slow, low monologue: she addressed the faces on the wall in friendly tones, prayed, sometimes, or reminisced, told libellous tales of the people of the town. I lay back against her in that state of greedy physical luxuriance only children can properly practise, with the castle above my head and the gallery of larger-than-lifes on equal and intimate terms, believing my grandmother to be a woman of truly mythic proportions.

This room of my memory contained, apart from icons, many very lovely and enchanting objects. First of all there was an abundance of expensive lace — on the backs of chairs, spread over the bed and the table, hung in corners of the room, even dangling from the lampshade — this compensated, Nina claimed, for a laceless childhood. It gave the room an appearance of frippery which always seemed to me rather at odds with the more serious and tasteful pictures on the wall. There was also a collection of hand-blown glass flower vases — perhaps twenty or more — arranged around the room. These usually stood empty, as exquisite ornaments, some carefully placed to catch light from the window. But on religious high days the flowers would arrive and the room became a kind of florist's dream; the vases bloomed bouquets of every conceivable type and shade. I remember now that there were also ornate candelabras, paperweights and jewels, and of course a Catholic saint or two crassly reincarnated as plaster monstrosities. And at the end of the bed, on a small antique chest of burnished rosewood, lay a stack of my comic books. Nina was illiterate but shared my fanatical pleasure in illustrations and super-heroes. We spent many happy hours reclined on her couch enjoined in the adventures of the Portuguese Spiderman.

Now let me tell you what happened. Nina, to put it frankly, was not of our class. She had been a 'varina', what in English you call a fishwife. My grandfather married her against custom because of her beauty and my father, a proud man, was very ashamed of his mother. Nina liked to embarrass him in company by displaying her fishing knowledge, by speaking in the language of the harbour, and sometimes by pulling me between her gigantic breasts in a way her son thought unseemly and rather vulgar. They always argued loudly and on one occasion he stormed into her room to pick a fight over something, and swung into a fury, sending two glass vases to glittering smithereens and decapitating a little statue of St Anthony of Padua. (St Anthony, needless to say, was Nina's favourite saint, being both Portuguese born and alleged to have preached to a school of fish.) Nina threw me from her, leaped up from the couch, and began shouting obscenities. She was so filled up with noisy anger that I thought the very haloes of the Holy would be set atrembling, that the Madonna would turn her pretty shocked face, that Christ himself would fearfully flinch.

But none of the pictures changed disposition; the outcome of the argument — it was so very sudden, and even now it upsets me — was that Nina disappeared. Father said she had gone mad and was recovering in hospital, but I never saw her again after the drama of that day. I waited and I waited, waited even as the objects in her room were gradually sold or taken away, refusing the evidence of my own sad eyes. Without Nina's presence, or rather with her absence, the room became intolerable. After a while I didn't even bother to climb the stairs; I stayed down in the shadows and tried to forget she had ever existed.

About a year later we moved to live in Lisbon, a move I have always attributed to my father's guilt. New school chums would say, 'Ah, Sintra, the castles!', and I would respond with bravado fantasies about ghosts and warriors and screams from the windows. I would describe with accuracy the Castelo da Pena at the peak of the mountain, and then fill it to the brim with furious kings, headless saints, demented mistresses, spider-limbed heroes. I was extremely popular, as you can imagine. But all the while I was thinking of Nina's room, of its pictures and vases and extravagant lace.

And then there came a moment — I recall it exactly — when I remembered a particular, unusual word Nina had one day used to describe the light in her room. 'Ardentia', she said, lifting back the curtain, standing, expansive, in a broad ray of silver twilight. Ardentia is a certain strange phosphorescence on the bodies of fish that fishermen learn to see on moonless nights. Her own grandfather, she told me, had taken her on a night cruise when she was very, very small just to see this legendary marine phenomenon. 'Ardentia.' At that moment of recollection I suddenly wept, since it replaced me on the spot, in her arms, beneath the mantilla — this state I had believed irrevocable — with the breath of her speaking, ever so soft and airy, down the back of my neck.

Patrick: The place I am thinking of is a small, out-of-the-way beach resort which I visited as a child for thirteen consecutive summers.

We lived in Melbourne where my father worked as an accounting clerk in an office in the city. We were quite a large family — I had four older brothers — so that we were, as my mother insisted, 'decently poor', living in the inner city in a 'decently shabby' semi-detached house. Our neighbours, as it happened, were a family of five daughters, similarly aged; this coincidence produced a childhood full of cinematically confected expectations of romance, tales of secret dalliances, crossings and criss-crossings of affection and regard, relentless flirtation, impossible desire. The whole neighbourhood seemed to delight in our statistically unlikely symmetry: matches were forecast by amused old ladies; scurrilous jokes were told by adolescents; visitors invariably remarked.

My brothers, I know, took great pride in these circumstances; indeed it later became the basis for their inflated reputations as local casanovas. But I found the entanglement — which was, in any case, mostly based on lies — very troubling and confining. I felt as if my life were threaded in and knotted to the family of girls, that somehow certain decisions had already been made without my agreement, that I had been caught in a design not of my own making. I watched my mother nightly embroider her industrious way over faint brown-inked lines and believed this was how it was: that I was sewn, bound, and predisposed. This belief somehow included the idea that I would never ever escape our tiny house, that I would be stuck forever sharing a cramped room with others and longing always for little moments of peace and quiet.

I should not overstate. Most of the time I was approximately happy, and was even, as predicted, an especial and close friend of the youngest neighbour. (Her name was Maria and we shared a keen interest in collecting postage stamps.) But it was the condi-

tions of our home life that made our annual visit to the beach so very important.

Since the year of his marriage my father had rented the same beach house for the same two weeks each and every January. This beach house was old, brilliantly whitewashed, and comprehensively comfortable. It had three small bedrooms, and also a wide-latticed, dog-rose entwined, part falling-to-pieces verandah where, in the domestic economy of redistributed bodies (and to my great pleasure), I was allotted a space. Here against the lattice I slept on a stretcher bed under a hanging mosquito net. Entering the net — this is how I always thought of it — was like creeping indecently under the skirts of some movie star dancer, so flimsy and cosseting and feminine were its folds. But it was a place of encompassing privacy and inertia. In the bleach-bright net I was singular, alone, removed from my brothers who fought in noisy pairs for the upper bunk in each bedroom, removed, more importantly, from the dim house in the city in which, apart from physical discomfort and sibling contestations, there were always high-pitched girl voices issuing in annoying streamers through the too-thin walls.

At night, I remember, I lay awake in the dark for as long as possible. Sleeping half outside was something of an adventure. The sky was very loud with the sound of the sea. Frisky possums skittered in rascal-packs across the roof. And through the superimposition of net and lattice I could see black bobbing rose-heads, trees wind-stirred into hideous shapes, and further, beyond that, a luminous ceiling of nameable stars. When I finally slept it was with these several dark dimensions rising and capsizing, depending on focus, through the layers of the night.

From the very moment I arrived at the summer beach house I began to feel released from my sewn up life. In the first place the pattern of our daily living changed. My mother, her appearance altered by a sun hat she wore only in our January fortnight, no longer prepared meals by the rigorous clock, but became gastronomically inconsistent and explorative. Meals were at all hours and likely to come labelled as 'Monday Surprise' or 'Wednesday Magic'. And she no longer sewed — stitches for pennies — but stretched relaxed on a wicker chair engrossed in magazines which bore smiling women's faces. My father, too, was markedly changed. A man of reticence and regularity, he would stay up late, sleep in, consume alcohol, enlargen, become talkative, friendly, almost accessible; he would dispatch, in short, his city-office self. We were all thus emancipated; our bodies returned to us more definitely sensual, as though we had been shades or Melbourne-embalmed; we remembered how to swim, how to run, how to shout; I tumbled with my brothers on warm subsiding sand, placed my body beside others in the full canary sunlight, slept long and dream-full and wholly languorous.

Yet the most profound change — for me, in any case — occurred in the sea, in the particular little bay at which we daily swam. As I sank my body in, watching goosebumps arise on flesh becoming blue, gasping from the cold of it — for which, after so many summers, I was still never quite prepared — feeling the inundation of every skin surface, both public and private, I imagined a state of physical dissolution. I imagined that the invisible threads by which I was bound unravelled through the water and were taken by currents, that filaments or skeins trailed away from my body — not, I should say, as if I were some sea-going creature, such as this sounds, but as a mystical being, spool-fashioned and exhilarated. I imagined that I was cleansed and wonderfully renewed. This belief was such that my daily run from the beach house to the sea, through teatree and paperbarks, past rocks to the sand, was filled with a more delicious sense of anticipation than I have ever since experienced. The submersion that followed was slow and solemn, up till the point, that is, when fraternal splashing and horseplay would invade my imagining.

So there was the house with its verandah and the sea with its renewal. Year after year we regularly returned; I came to think of the holiday as a kind of incorruptible, bright, cellophane-shiny space in which were distilled only those qualities that countered the city. My life, I thought, subtended always to that point, those two weeks elsewhere, those unencumbered, sea-washed, net-embraced, two weeks.

The twelfth summer, however, was different from the rest. Our first week was as usual — I was still on the verandah, still swam, still played. But in the second week there were bushfires somewhere to the west, so that for three whole days the sky was dense with suspended ash. Ash fell in fine sprinkles on the roses over the verandah, it coated the furniture and we could taste it on our tongues. The air became brownish and the sun recoloured an ugly rust red. But worse than this, far worse to my child-mind, was that ash also fell pervasively upon the sea. Waves were dark fringed and ash was deposited in scallop shaped tidal lines all along the beach. I remember that my brothers ran around the bay, scooping up handfuls of the filthy stuff and flinging it at each other, while I stood and stared, utterly dumbfounded, at the sullied sea water. Yet—and this is the strange thing — I still thought it important, vitally important, to swim. To miss even a day would be to destroy the ritual repetition upon which my holiday was founded.

So eventually I walked into the impure sea, I, alone among my brothers, and duly submerged. I did not unravel. I did not transform into unwinding glory. I did not cast off my parents, or the girls next door, or my stupid-seeming brothers. I stayed tight and wound up and when I arose my skin was stained and explicitly polluted. Around me the sun had broken into scarlet fragments that rocked against my body. Particles of ash swam up to adhere to me. The water stank. My brothers called from the shore in mocking voices and I could see my mother in her sun hat move to the middle distance beside the rocks to see what was going on. So it was, that day, that I did not actually cry — since I could not at all bear the thought of witness — but swam into shore pretending to be wholly unaffected and untouched. Yet the swill of ash would later recur in nightmares, terribly multiplied, as a drowning sludge, viscid, suffocating and final.

The thirteenth summer was entirely clean. I thoughtlessly enjoyed myself, not knowing that the visit to the beach house would be my last, that the owner would sell it in the following spring.

My fourteenth summer was thus spent at our house in the city, miserable in exile, bisected in spirit, and dreaming of a seaside which returned contradictorily both in consoling memories and awful nightmares, a seaside which had once, just once, been horribly contaminated, but which was before and ever after absolutely pure.

Narrator: The place which I will tell you about is really my sister's place, for it was she who discovered it, she who boldly claimed it as personal and private, she who appointed it with lavish, fantastic, invisible decorations, spun from the munificence of her own daredevilish mind. No introverted soul, she flung out whimsy and visions as other children do chatter; she was larger-than-life, astonishing, an addict of novelties. I loved her, of course, as she commanded to be loved, with exceeding passion.

The place Anna discovered was a cave at the very edge, the very boundary, of our property. My parents owned a dairy farm in the south-west of Western Australia; it was small and unprofitable, and stood precariously on ancient limestone that reached deep below the earth in a series of caverns and chambers. My father told stories of how, in the past, cattle had been swallowed whole and in one hungry gulp by the treacherous, disguised hollows of his patch of land, but always added — with due parental regard for the not-too-frightening — that all was now safer and much more stable. Nevertheless he warned us never to investigate new depressions or unfamiliar, unusual chinks or cavities: these, my father announced (tapping his pipe in a gesture of emphasis), were the swallowing kind, the mouth to look out for.

I trod the soil twice daily with my older sister as we brought in the cows for milking at dawn and at dusk. My feet were unsure. I lived for many years — until, in fact, the discovery of the cave — with the belief that I might one day precipitously be claimed by an instant hole, that I might suddenly fall away into an awful, oral darkness, and never be recovered. (Anna was not bothered by such terrestrial threats; in fact she was a child of apparently no fears at all, convinced of her own invincible tangibility.)

Yet I enjoyed the farm. Our house was set low in a slight valley or declension so that around us rose paddocks unfolding in a vista of mounds and undulations, creek channels and gullies, all of which were spotted with immobile looking cows and over-hung and over-

seen by drifting hawks. The paddocks were green and pungent with dung, the cows black and white, the hawks an indefinite aerial brown. Red gums and sheoaks stood in isolated native patches: fences perspectivally trailed. There was a glistening dam, and a few large rocky outcrops. A wooden milking shed quaintly showed dilapidation; another, newer and of corrugated iron, housed a hire-purchase tractor.

So lovely and specific in re-creation, this farmscape existed then as the unobtrusive circumstance, the mere daily condition, of my childhood life. (Like many rural born I know my home more exactly with excommunication.) I moved through its features barely aware, charmed, perhaps, but also largely indifferent, and with only the risk of a plunge disturbing my habitual unreflection.

Anna, I believe, was more observant than I. It was she, that day, who pointed with an ah ha! at the rocks near the boundary. We were upon our horses, inspecting the fences, but finding fencelines too strict and boringly imperative, Anna had trotted off southwards on some slight deviation into an area of wild scrub. When she called me to join her I was confronted with the history book posture of white explorers: Anna, still mounted, sat stiff on her horse with her arm extended and a finger firmly pointed in expeditionary certainty. This image I retain of her — humorous, bold, replete with instinctive satire; more particularly a ring of light just so on her yellow hair, a face unable to suppress its grin, spatters of shadow on the theatrical arm, and the horse, the necessary addition to so many of her games, heaving its sides slightly but otherwise obediently still.

The hole in the rocks I knew at once to be terrible. It was the precise apparition my father had described, not a walk-in room but a sneaky dark aperture, a going nowhere tunnel, a body-sized orifice. To my great alarm Anna hastily dismounted, threw herself headfirst into the rocky hole and wriggled quickly away, her feet following immediately like scrabbling little animals. I burst into tears — as I was wont to do — and begged and begged and begged her to return. I screamed into the hole and reached in my arms, hoping to snatch at a retreating toe. Whereupon, after apparently interminable distress, Anna duly returned, again headfirst, her dirty face smiling at my shameful display.

It was weeks before Anna persuaded me underground. Each time she took torches, books, candles and food, and I waited, excluded, on the lonely surface. Bound to absolute secrecy — by an exchange of blood squeezed from pinpricks to the thumbs on the stroke of midnight — I was privately miserable, sequestered away in my foolish and untellable fear. And when I finally descended it was with a rope around my waist so that I would not fall away forever to the centre of the earth, but be caught by a tree-hold and able to climb out.

After a slanting, constricted, knee-scraping belly crawl the cave itself was unexpectedly spacious. It rose to a vault from which young stalactites and sinuous plant roots depended. The walls were partly of earth and partly of rock, so that the sense of containment was not, as I had imagined, tight and sculptured, but rather pleasantly burrowish, with a sweet scent of vegetable life moderating the musk of mineral lime. It was also vaguely lit — Anna's candles and torches had implied to me pitch blackness — by a space in the ceiling through which a lucent spot of sky was clearly visible, a spot which, for its tiny size, conveyed a disproportionate quantity of fluctuating blue light.

Into this special enclosure we emptied ourselves. In this secret cave, this secret receptacle, so far from the tap of our father's pipe, we fashioned playtimes and stories with exuberant skill and preternatural pleasure. Anna was a genius of nonsense and invention. She was a performing chatter-box, silly, burlesque, endlessly entertaining. I sat in the half dark and watched, captivated, as my sister danced and revolved around me, a human cinema, a cluster of characters, a congregation of worlds all completely compelling. Anna's voices were louder tied in by convexity, her body much larger rescaled by compartment. She achieved in our cave that gift of multiplicity, that high pitch of largesse, for which actors of all kinds persistently strive.

The farm became changed with the advent of the secret — a secret which, by the way, Anna called Our Den Of Iniquity. I was no longer afraid of the swallowing earth; rather I imagined that we trod over dozens of perfect hollows, a honeycomb of dwellings which were the residences of creatures ebullient as children, but in other ways indescribable. And the shape of the farm seemed also to change. I looked out of my window up the slopes of the paddocks, past the static cows and the lazy wooded creek, and imposed upon the land, from a hawk's eye view, a neat triangulation to the point of the cave. This private geography I nightly rehearsed; before I lay beside my sister I would gaze into the dark, reconstruct swift diagonals and a pointy apex, and bid the hidden cave a succinct goodnight.

Anna was just twelve, and I only nine, when she died. She overturned a tractor and was instantly broken. My parents buried their daughter beside the house, fulfilling both the stringencies of poverty and their own fervent atheism.

All the long, lonely, Anna-less years of my adolescence I continued to visit Our Den Of Iniquity. Anna's hieroglyphics remained chalked upon the wall, still indecipherably Egyptian. Her dress-ups and books stayed unmoved on the floor. Her feathers, her marbles, her magnifying glass, her sketches, these tokens of solidarity with the world of substance, all remained crudely and disloyally in existence. Her fantastic life gone, the cave forfeited, in response, its most congenial aspects — of the rambunctious and the ridiculous, of the higgledy-piggledy, the hugger-mugger, the harum-scarum. And when I lay in the half dark, with the little spot of light directly above my head, I did not dare replace Anna there in the secret cave, now so sad, so dismal, so sister-deprived, but instead reversed my imagining so that the vectors of my mind-map extended back in converging lines to the grave beside the house, her new underground, her body-sized cave, back where, thinking very hard with my eyes tightly closed, I sought and sought her skidaddled soul.

When we finished our stories we lay back in the dark. Night insects could be heard. The breeze had increased and seemed to bring with it a visible increase in blackness. Later, when they thought me safely and soundly asleep, I heard Patrick and Afonso move close enough to embrace.

And in my lonely singularity I contemplated the connection between us all, the connection of space, the connection of narrative. As I heard Patrick's lips upon Afonso's body (or was it vice versa?), I tried to imagine the ways in which the individual kiss and all its individualising implications might be installed and respected in the larger occurrences of a country's history. And simply could not.

V

Do you know this history? Let me be brief. From August to December 1975 East Timor was governed defacto by the popularly supported Fretlin movement.

East Timor declared itself independent on the twenty-eighth of November: nine days later Indonesia unexpectedly invaded, engaged war with the local people and took control.

In the next eighteen months of conflict one hundred thousand people, or one-sixth of the population, were killed.

Portugal was preoccupied with internal affairs. Its army and its people were riven in revolutionary and counter-revolutionary contestation.

Requests for diplomatic help from Australia against unprovoked aggression and the denial of national self-determination were met with dithering disengagement. East Timor was unimaginable and therefore considered inconsequential.

Fretlin fighters were driven to the vaccinated highlands where they engaged (knowing the cliffs and rivers, the serpentine roads) in guerilla warfare. They lost.

Patrick Donelly, my friend, was with a group of five Australian journalists who, seeking frontline dispatches in that miserable territory, were confronted in a surprised moment by Indonesian machine-guns only to discover, pathetically, that no protestations of nationality deflected bullets. His brutalised body was burned in a pit. He was reduced to ash with dozens of others, who, though still remaining nameless to outside intelligence, were no less loved, no less specific, and no less precious than he.

Afonso Vieira, hearing the news from the safety of his Portuguese villa, sent me a letter of grief smudged over by apparently unrestrainable tears. A year later a note arrived from the city of Sintra, the city of castles. It was from an old friend of Afonso and stated, with rather too strict a tone of impersonality, that he had committed suicide.

VI

Sometimes in the summer I wear my Timorese sarong and think of the women in the stone market place who through some intrinsic dignity and the extra aid of narcotics resisted the misappropriating gaze of the soldiers. This continues to preoccupy me, the evidence of resistance, this imperturbable solidity.

I remember that, as a tourist, I wore a pair of reflecting sunglasses by which I carried, with bland incomprehension, doubled images of the country in little screens upon my face. Doubled highlands. Doubled soldiers. Doubled peasants or *mauberes*.

I remember too that there were masses of purple bougainvillea in severely bright light. There were pockmarked buildings on the verge of disintegration, jungles, wild deer, Fretlin supporters on trucks, a statue of the Virgin colonially dislocated, a certain doctor's face.

And there is another small detail which I irresistibly recall, but pause to include since it seems too obscurely symbolic for this fact-seeking prose. Yet it is a detail of precisely that clarity of punctilious emplacement that I long to record.

There is a bridge in the centre of the Eastern half of Timor which is incomplete. This is not to say that the builders did not finish their work, nor that it collapsed in some area or other. Rather, there are two concrete arcs — designed in Portugal by map-consulting engineers — which begin on each bank of a broad brown river, stretch forward to meet, both in their strong bows, but then, through some stupid or unfortunate miscalculation of space, fail entirely to join. In the dry season this monumental mistake is ignored, since the riverbed is empty, and one may walk safely across the absent water. But when the wet season comes flimsy ferries are employed, and each year people drown, are swept swiftly seawards under the concrete arms, cursing as they go.

The Precision of Angels

Mary's mother was a Literalist. Nightly she bent above the Book, halo-ringed and brightened by her desk lamp.

She pursued substance. She sought the verifiable. She read, and in reading conferred actual existence, rendered words responsible. Her hand slid down and across each light-white page, tracing with sure fingertips the neatly sequential lines of the real. Entities arose. Events. Essences. Nothing was dubious. In the long dark hours, so otherwise unsure, so filled with intimations of unGodly appetites, truant devotions and unspeakable acts, Mary's mother was wed to the true.

The crescent moon elevated, opaque clouds sped, stars began unwinding their Heavenly revolutions.

In her fortieth year, when her daughter, then eleven, became afflicted with epilepsy, Mary's mother began to specialise in the study of angels. The vision Mary presented was too shocking to ignore: it was a vision of creatureliness. The child's body convulsed and her limbs became errant. A sweet face was remade in a series of contractions and contortions. Violence of some kind agitated crudely and extensively in every physical space, muscles, chambers, the very planes of the skin.

Astonished at this unseemly and unprecedented aberration, this triumph of Devilish caricature over innocent solemnity, Mary's mother sought out a scriptural explanation. She knelt beside her daughter — who was still heaving her mind out of her wracked condition, bruised, abased, bleeding slightly from the tongue, moist and stained with her own leaked urine — and declared with certainty a theory of visitation.

It may be, she suggested, following the theories of St Jerome, the work of fallen angels who, unlike their more righteous and ethereal cousins, have bodies of damp air and visit inconveniently and with malicious purpose. Then again, she pronounced, it may be an angel of the avenging kind. As the Book of Kings attests, one single angel is able to exterminate overnight a whole army of Assyrian warriors; but there are of course many recorded cases of lesser molestation. Either way, she continued, you must undertake penance, since such obvious punishment shows you definitely to be sinful.

Mary lay on the floor looking up at the unconsoling face of her mother and behind her a windowful of changing night. She thought to herself how little she knew, how empty she was of knowledge and understanding. But she knew this much: that nothing of her condition verged upon the metaphysical, unless it be the glimpses of forewarning stars lit randomly in her head. These stars blazed up, momentarily scintillated, and then were eclipsed by a flood of blood and the bold spasms of seizure. Mary did not tell her mother of the presence of the stars; she held it a secret within her, private, precious.

Mary's mother spoke of angels with pedantic precision. As she attacked her spaghetti she told her daughter the details of their modes of locomotion.

Of the nine orders of angels, she pronounced between mouthfuls, the seraphim, the highest order, are likely to be the swiftest. According to Isaiah they are equipped with six wings, two on the face, two on the feet, and two with which they principally fly. Remember, however, that as spiritual essence, angels do not take up any space.

At her mother's description Mary smiled to herself. Unlike the usual tales of plague and revenge, sin and catastrophe, this one seemed to indicate an order of comic plenitude. She imagined a being, miraculously spaceless, stepping from a luminous backdrop of winking stars. It was pompously unangelic, being stuck all over with the still-flapping bodies of a dozen glued birds. One bird had alighted on the back of the head, and cupped the obscure face like outsized ears.

She cherished this image as children cherish, before adults, their own lies and misdemeanours.

After a difficult attack Mary opened her eyes to find her mother very close and anxiously inquisitive.

Are there voices? she asked. You must tell me about voices.

Mary closed her eyes. She felt her skin becoming livid with its past exertions, felt the embarrassing wet, the pain, the dishevelment. She was inordinately tired, and wished only to lapse into dream-vacant sleep. But she heard her mother's voice imperiously continue:

St Paul, of course, speaks of the 'tongues of angels', but there is some keen dispute as to their means of communication. They can address humans intelligibly, as Gabriel did at the Annunciation, but otherwise may talk by pure intelligence. According to St Thomas angels open their minds to each other in a perfectly mutual and wordless revelation. Does your angel speak? Is it in English? Latin?

Mary feared to look, knowing she would see what she saw at first, her own prostrate form, swimming, doubled, tinily reduced, in the globes of her mother's interrogative eyes.

Mary's mother began dying in her fiftieth year. No less Literal than before, she lay back on her bed — having refused a hospital — and awaited angelophany, an angelic manifestation.

There are so many, she said; the prophet Daniel speaks of thousands upon tens of thousands. Surely one will be spared to guide me Home.

She continued with her Book, her finger careful and specific beneath each single word, her eyes tight and concentrated in an industrious squint. When the pain became too great Mary read to her mother, and as night drew on she positioned the desk lamp so that it brilliantly illuminated the text.

I may visit you when dead, the mother said one night. St Frances of Rome, who died in 1440, saw her dead son Evangelista return as an angel. He had remarkable hair, composed of a flaming, holy, incisive light, right down to his shoulders. His mother could not look at him without hurting her eyes, but was ecstatic at his visits. She was able to read her Bible by the hair's resplendent glow, and its light was such that it enabled her to know the thoughts of men around her, and to understand all the devious machinations of the Devil.

Mary looked down at her mother, who had become grey and shrivelled with approaching death, and was unable to conceive of any illustrious return. Thin ashen hair fell in trails on the pillow. The face was reduced, barely still her mother but some stranger who had stolen her mother's voice. The stranger died unvisited, murmuring in whispered fragments that the angel who deigned to visit St Francis of Assisi carried in its hands an ancient violin.

After the long slow death, daughter Mary divorced her past and sought her own recuperation in the consolations of the flesh. She undertook a career of earnest concupiscence, finding with men a derangement of the senses unexpectedly pleasurable.

It was a night full of stars when the event occurred. Her lover moved in the dark, skilfully attentive, supple, fluent, tacit and tongue-gentle. He touched and he entered and as she spread apart her thighs she felt the concurrent and interior beginnings of a flutter of featherlife. Wings began to beat and blood to rush and for a second Mary thought that her epilepsy had returned. But the wings continued uplifting, a rhythm, a flight, until, without a doubt, horizons subsided and the angel was entrenched. There was a luxurious suffusion, a voluptuous loss of breath, so special as to be certainly, quintessentially celestial. Mary heard herself panting with the force of possession, felt the translucencies of the life of the sky, felt the breeze of another presence ebb and dissolve.

When her lover switched on the lamp and knelt beside her at the bed Mary saw her own image. In the limpid hemispheres of his beautiful eyes she was doubly floating: glorious, naked, almost beatific. And before her, outside, splendid and far, was an extensive realm of space now wholly sidereal.

The angels known as seraphim, she whispered very low, are

generously endowed. They have three pairs of wings, one on the face, one on the feet, and one with which they spacelessly speed.

Dark Times

I am not courageous. Now that the country is brimful of assassins I lie awake at night. I start at shadows. I fear the phone. The faces of friends appear furtive and changed. A smear of blood in the hallway, crimson as rose-flourish and oddly indelible, augurs huge alterations.

The meetings of our group were always rather small. They consisted of a few of my graduate students, most of whom were working away at irrelevant theses (and thus, in the narrow range of student temperaments, either studiously earnest, arrogant or shy), and my fellow historian M (temperamentally all three and, engaged as he was in a perpetual project of indefinite scope, similarly word-burdened). We bent over documents and considered them together.

As scandals go this was insubstantial. A local politician had siphoned off funds intended for road works. He was related, of course, to the ruling family, and possessed, of course, a private militia. In addition he conformed to the familiar caricature, khaki-and-dark-glasses, copiously bodied, nasty, brutish and rather short. He was, that is, nothing unusual at all, a codified personification, formulaic, severe.

Yet I recall, that night, that I seemed actually to apprehend this politician's presence in my room. Fear curiously substantiates. We sat close together in our small bulb-lit circle, clustering like conspirators in some cinema classic, and he might almost have been present as a seventh member. And if he sat anywhere he sat beside me: I could sense the space at my elbow claimed and inhabited; I could feel the hairs of his invisible arm brush ever so softly, like a contagion, against mine; I could hear, or so I thought, the very beat of his terrible heart. The smoke of his cigar joined our cigarette haze; his hot breath commingled. The State of Emergency had produced this effect, had rendered incarnate evils otherwise removed at the image-safe distance of newspaper photographs and billboards.

We paused at our work for black tea and pitted dates, but the palpable presence did not dispel.

When the door burst open I was almost unstartled. Men with batons swung in through the room, bringing with them the sudden taut urgency of accidents. The light globe swung too, taking our shadows into monstrous elongations, sliding dark, elastic phantoms up and down the walls. I watched my own form rush back towards me, and waited, impassively, to be struck out by steel.

Tea tipped and spilt; a brass tray spun skywards.

They took only M. After a few bold concussions they took only M. From terror or bravery he had remained in his chair, but they seized him instantly upwards and sent him hurtling away. His body fell through the doorway and came to rest heavily inanimate and askew in the hall. His head had exploded in a crimson rose-flourish. He was perfectly still. Then the men efficiently bundled their limp, bloody bundle, and were gone.

When the wide-swinging light came finally to rest I could still sense a presence stirring air at my elbow. But the panting I heard, so thick and inhuman, was only my own.

I remember Cambridge. I was younger then. I walked between stone and trees and bright glassy shops and was utterly disbelieving. The English amazed me. Clothes. Manners. Their stiffened smiles. Their strict punctuality. The men with hands perpetually in pockets. The women with hats and hard-substanced handbags. I thought for a time that I was the only one real, that the population I moved in was white enough for ghosts and almost as insipid, but in the end was persuaded by their solidity of touch. After books and study and long nights alone I submitted my colour to the tremulous affections of many pale fingers. Both women and men. On moonlit sheets I cast back my body; I reclined, was embraced, and became the exotic by which they generally defined me. I confirmed passivity or surprised with novelties; I assumed the many and various forms of my figurative foreignness.

By day radiant pages flicked fan-like before me, their words neat and black, and absolutely certain.

In this tense waiting time it is difficult to read and almost impossible to write. The journals of my discipline begin to repel me. For all this country's chaos mail doggedly continues; history journals, new books and sky-blue lettergrams still fly across the ocean to land upon my desk as though nothing had changed.

Today at the riot there were five television cameras. Tomorrow my friends in England will see a scramble of people, a few swift trucks and the distant advertisement of guns. (Crowd scenes, military, perhaps a number of conscientious and shocking brutalities.) In the casual and lazy fraternity of pubs they will imagine adventure. Several will write lines on sky-blue paper to express solidarity. More will turn instead to the comprehendible horrors of the late night movie.

I shuffle my books in simulation of work. I fiddle with papers and scribble a paragraph. The very word 'history' begins to torment me. I change and re-change, unable to concentrate, my article on subaltern class formations. From outside comes the acrid smell of burning cars, and, somewhere within it, persistent traces of musky incense drifting upwards from the temple.

Darkness descends. I fear the darkness. Outside beggars bed down under blankets of cardboard. From my window I can see them nestling in tight little corners, or snuggling, paper enclosed, against the walls of this building. They curl up like commas and hope for dreams.

Since M has been taken nights are almost unendurable.

It is foolish, really, the things one remembers. I was seated in a cafe, playing colonial-acting-English, on a day, I recall, untypically static and warm. It was the day of my very first Devonshire tea. Such sumptuous blandness!: the scones plump and dusty with a coating of flour, the jam shinily viscous and chemical red, and there, on the splendid willow-pattern plate, a huge mound of cream. The tea was presented in a miniature teapot of fine beaten silver; beside it stood a jug and bowl similarly fashioned and lit for the occasion by a stream of lemon sunlight. The domestic aesthetics were most alluring. I plunged at the scones with unwarranted greediness.

The topic of my thesis in English history at Cambridge was 'Documentary responses to the Peterloo massacre'. On the sixteenth of August 1819 almost sixty thousand working men and women (plus sundry attendant children and domestic pets) met at St Peter's Field on the outskirts of Manchester for a peaceful demonstration in the cause of radical reform. The scene was, by all accounts, one of manifold pageantry. Banners bore slogans proclaiming 'Liberty and Fraternity', 'Votes for Women', 'Unity and Strength' and 'Parliaments Annual, Suffrage Universal'. One dog, it is recorded, carried the words 'No Dog Tax' hung decoratively at its neck. The crowd was orderly and unarmed and feeling somewhat festive. Women in white bonnets grew brave with ideas. Men became loud and happily animate. There were greetings and discussions and hail-ye-well-mets. A maid received, unnoticed, a kiss from her admirer. The dog with its sign snoozed at somebody's feet. A baby drank slowly at a cushion of breast.

On the orders of the magistracy — so it is written — the local yeomanry charged into the crowd with their horses, intent upon the speaker, a man called Hunt. The baby was trampled; the speaker seized. The crowd grew angry and began to jeer. The Yeomanry panicked and drew their swords and then Mounted Hussars intervened to aid the Yeomanry. An energetic ten minute slaughter ensued. Eleven were killed. Four hundred and twenty-one were seriously injured; one hundred and sixty-two (including women and children) bore evidence of sabre wounds. St Peter's Field, initially so bright and carnivalesque, was completely deserted, littered in retreat with dropped caps, shawls, banners and shoes, and densely marked with a pattern of semi-circular declensions that showed in the soil the agitations of the horses.

I remember devouring scones as I totalled up casualties. I sat in the cafe and spread my books before me, savouring, in part, the sweet aspect of discrepancy between the pleasures of my feast and the unfortunate, woebegone miseries of the past.

R has phoned to say that she and the others are moving underground. They request that I join them.

I have noticed that the telephone, in its particular, technological distortion of voices, tends not to affirm the presence of people but remove them further away than they could possibly be. R's voice hung somewhere in distant space; it was loose and unearthly. I had joked on this before, but it now seemed she inhabited a somewhere utterly unimaginable.

You must come right away, she whispered in English. We will meet you at eight at the place we agreed on.

It was as though she was proposing to travel through light years of dark, past planets and stars and speeding meteors, just to meet up with me.

I will come, I lied, unconvinced of her existence.

Upon hearing the news of the Peterloo massacre the Romantic poet Shelley wrote *The Mask of Anarchy.* In a sparkling glass tower at Villa Valsovano in pretty Livorno he took up his pen. The poem is spare and metrical and too well rhymed (following the fashion of the time), and tells the tale, rather abstractly, of St Peter's Field. Against the sabres and bayonets of the class-bound State, it urges passive resistance.

Stand ye calm and resolute
Like a forest close and mute
With folded arms and looks which are
Weapons of unvanquished war...

The poem was not published in the poet's lifetime; no publisher would risk gaol for its blatant sedition.

In this difficult time I distract myself by re-reading *The Mask of Anarchy*. Here, in my own country, I imaginatively rehearse an English atrocity of 1819. I cannot encounter unmediated the reality of worse events in the streets outside. I am overcome by the idiotic melodrama of recitation, by the fact of repetition, either as tragedy or farce, around which my own anxieties centre and turn. Like an unmotivated automaton I spin out words, seeking, in this sad act, some semblance of comfort.

Images of Cambridge continue to assail me. As I lie awake at night I see the past re-presented: the languid Cam with its streaming threads of green slime, its obese grey swans, its false Venetians; the silhouetted and multiple spires of Kings College; silent bicycles weaving down dark winding streets, donnish groups in conversation, over-stocked bookshops, picturesque teahouses. I contemplate its facade of manners and rectitude, its smug self-enclosure, its apoliticism. And I think, half in reverie, of sexual encounters, of lovers — one in particular — with whom, in my studenthood, nationless and irresponsible, I sought dissipation.

I had a terrible dream. It began calmly. I was alone on a couch, reclined and insouciant. A book lay face downwards somewhat heavily on my chest; I had just finished reading. It was one of those dream moments entirely plausible, as though some chunk of waking life had infracted accidentally and lodged itself in sleep. I was comfortable and composed, the scholar recumbent. But then, without warning, the light bulb in my room began swinging large arcs. The walls began to fill with shadows of invisible people. I felt my heart arouse, waiting for the fearful strike of steel. But instead of hard blows I began, inexplicably, to be smothered by paper. The book on my chest had transformed into cardboard and it lay with a suffocating weight against my lungs. I could feel myself being cancelled, becoming flattened, negligible.

I awoke sucking in anguish at the cold night-time air.

My supervisor at Cambridge was a gentleman, it was said, of impeccable humanity. That is to say he took sherry with his students and spoke earnestly and sincerely of the benefits and rewards of a liberal arts education. As I sat in his shaded, oak-panelled room, surrounded by the required contingent of leather bound volumes glinting gold titles, I believed for a moment that I had reached the very summit of Western civilisation. I contemplated the garnet swaying in its glass, smelt its alcoholic odour in the instant before I sipped, and thought to myself: this is how it should be, this leisure, this repose, this oak-and-leather ambience.

The old man leaned slowly forward — I remember it well — and asked me, in the most genial and patient of tones, to describe the institutes of higher education which existed in my country. What was I to say? I looked down at my brown hands and recalled irresistibly only those features of my home that were rude and inexpressible: the press of thin bodies in a crowded market place, garments blowing brightly in dark, narrow doorways, spiced food cooked outside on pathetically doll-sized burners, the stench of human excrement, paraphernalia of brass, rumblings of bullock carts, altars, trinkets, familiar syllables. But I could not summon any kind of intelligent response. I heard myself stammer a few awkward and halting sentences about ethnographic difference, about infrastructural absences, about the indisputable, regrettable depredations of colonialism.

And then I noticed that the sherry glass had become tiny and very brittle in my large home-made hands.

On the walls beneath my window square posters have appeared. They show the media-wise politician, the one who used funds once intended for roadworks. He does not deign to smile, since in the convention of our country politicians appear stern; they must resemble in opacity and seriousness the statues they will inevitably erect. Nor does he stare; the eyes have been replaced by oblongs of dark glass. He has already achieved the eyeless and irreproachable equanimity of statuehood. I am reminded of Shelley's famous 1817 sonnet, *Ozymandias,* in which the shattered statue of a '*king of kings*' is discovered in a realm of boundless desert. On the surviving face of stone it is still possible to read '*the sneer of cold command*', though nothing at all remains of the empire and its authority.

Beggars continue to bed down against buildings. I find them

preoccupying. I watch their shapes curl and huddle and arrange large flaps of cardboard which, from this distance, look like the wings of black Harpies, settling hungrily over prey. Try as I may I cannot even imagine their emotions or thoughts. They are inscrutable as the servants who attended my childhood.

Gunshots ring out at some inestimable distance. There is an explosion to the west signified by a bow of illumination resting low in the smoky and oppressive sky.

I wanted so desperately to become an Englishman. More specifically I wanted to be Percy Bysshe Shelley: languorously privileged, poetically audacious, bright, sexual, famously young. Instead I set to work, there in my study, resolving to produce a volume on Peterloo to honour my history teacher. In it I would attest the superior exegetical powers of the historical mode. It would be a stunning approval of cause and effect, of the stringency of facts, of objective and disinterested scholarship.

I did not, as it happened, achieve my aim. The examiner's report — though in some ways praising — announced that this candidate had problems with expression in the English language (too florid by half) which, while not wholly constituting any failure or disqualification, would not, in the eventuality, recommend the text for publication...

I did publish, nevertheless, a small volume of mediocre poems titled *Personal and Political* and dedicated to my lover. I remember that I rushed through the streets with an extravagantly wrapped copy, holding it out like a kind of trophy before me, my words, my desires, all print-elegant and bound, until I arrived huffing and puffing and dishevelled by excitement. My lover glanced at the volume with an incurious stare. His slender white hands casually flicked at the pages. He said he was actually-awfully-busy-at-the-moment and would I care to return at a more satisfactory time.

They have come to arrest me. I cannot pretend I had not expected it. The files on Ozymandias were taken four days ago and my dissent is recorded in the very fact of their existence.

I am heaved outside into a waiting van. I pass beggars and posters, the former with all the diffidence and anonymity of the dispossessed, the latter familiar and strikingly specific. The night is very dark. Above me space stretches away to infinity and I find myself stupidly thinking that R is out there somewhere, that she is orbiting above, that she and the others are caught up in a realm of wheeling stars, are distant, lost, unrecoverable.

His slender white hands casually flicked at the pages. My book spun before me like a radiant fan. For you, I said; the love poems are for you. His beautiful eyelids slowly raised. I remember I thought his eyes particularly exquisite. He said he was actually-awfully-busy...

This prison is not at all as I expected. I had somehow imagined much noise and crowding but it is quiet and solitary. Perhaps I am kept in a section of the prison divorced from others. Perhaps this is a concession to the wealth of my family, to their past political influence. Nevertheless it is damp and unspeakably cold. My limbs have contracted, I am sure, with the effect of incessant shivering. I try to warm myself mentally. I think of garnet sherry in a short fluted glass. I think of Devonshire tea in a streak of sunlight, more precisely of the wavering steam above the tea, of the willow pattern plate, of the mound of cream, the lemon of the light. In my vision I inhabit a sparkling glass tower.

I prepared an excellent line of defence. I would argue that my interest in the politician Ozymandias was merely historical, that I was a member of no party, politically innocent, clean, pure. I would invoke the principle of impartiality in scholarship and argue the importance of documentation and research. I would cite my old teacher and wax eloquent both on the necessity of the discipline of history — its nationalistic benefits, its handy property of assimilation to any state ideology — and on the final ineffectuality of academic words.

But none of this worked. The man in military uniform who confronted me in my cell cut short my speech and simply laughed outright. Your crime, he said, is of sexual deviance. You are sexually corrupt; you have corrupted others. And then he did the most extraordinary thing. In the dialect of my district he began to recite, with a fine solemnity, one of my early love poems, one written twenty years ago for the lover, my lover, my long lost

English lover, who was actually-awfully-busy.

Maps are eradicable.
The place of your residence
has remade space. I think to myself
'he lives over there' and elsewhere
floats off as though wholly
uninhabited, mythical as Garuda
lifting such graceful and improbable wings.

Invisible is visible.
Absence does not seem
to diminish you at all. Here
in my room, so crammed and populous
with self-proclaiming curios,
fabrics from far lands, shells,
books, the desk with its papers,
you hover definitively. The very air
contains you. My potted flowers
quiver by the touch of your hand.
Your breath at the window,
your certain face.
The blind would say knowingly
'There are two people here'.

The military man paused at this point in his recitation and laughed once again. The rest, he said, is too dirty to say; and he turned and walked away, presumably taking the remainder of my poem, translated into dialect, and reeling to its lascivious conclusion in his head.

I cannot remember the rest of my poem. I keep repeating to myself the last uttered line 'There are two people here', in the hope that I will recuperate the lost direction of the words. I know that I fantasised the sexual act, that I joined with my conjured figment of a lover and embraced in some imaginary aspatial place. I know that my language became rich and romantic, that I lavishly described presence in absence. It was a poem of infatuation, naive, flagrant. My words, however, do not seem forthcoming. The poem of my youth is entirely forgotten.

I am so very, very cold and not at all courageous. This cell has a quality of ill-omen about it; it is dark and damp and filled with repugnant quantities of spiders and cockroaches. I think of the world that exists beyond this cell, the press of thin bodies in the crowded market place, garments blowing brightly in dark narrow doorways, spiced food cooked outside on pathetically doll-sized burners, the stench of human excrement, paraphernalia of brass, rumblings of bullock carts, colours, altars, trinkets, syllables. I think of beggars bedding down beneath sheets of cardboard. I think of the posters multiplying throughout the city, each image like the last, each face made eyeless, each repetition extending the infiltration of a man whom no one actually sees; of the dark sky arching above, of my friends lost and drifting in its airless depths. I think of smoke and gunfire and the blank gaze of cameras. Crowds rushing before tanks in a modernised Peterloo. The fallen, the crushed, the crimson rose-flourish.

Two men have unexpectedly brought M to my cell. He is naked and unconscious and his testicles have been burned by cigarettes. He is cast back on the stone floor like one already dead.

You next mister professor, says one of the men. He speaks, like the reciter, in the dialect of my area. His skin is exactly the colour of mine. His hair as black. His expression as imprecise.

M lays on the floor obscenely exposed. M's face has changed: it is no longer the face my lips explored, no longer preciously lover-familiar. It is barely, in fact, recognisable at all.

I walk to my burning not wanting to be Shelley. I walk to my burning simply wanting, more than anything, to recover the lost, modest memory of my poem, to return to the moment in which such things were tellable and such words possible, in which the liberties of the body were wider liberties, in which history was something sequestered, sedate and academically amenable. I keep saying to myself 'There are two people here', but beyond that nothing comes. Beyond that there is a terrible pandemonium of words which shift and change with no order or reference, which are anarchic and inconsequential, and which sound in my head as though they were spoken from deep space through all the coils and deviations of telephone wires. The past is lost. I feel weak and pathetic. Yet I say to myself, again and again, 'There are two people here'.

The Word 'Ruby'

(*De minimus non curat lex:* The law does not concern itself with trifles.)

Janet Allotson, barrister, of Hawthorn, Melbourne, had awoken with the force of a dislocating memory. She blinked into consciousness and found herself tumbled elsewhere, other age, other class, other time.

The morning-caught memory was one of striking lucidity: no enigmatic residue, no dream paraphrase, no unsystematic or circuitous flotsam and jetsam, but almost, one might say, a clear and distinct idea.

It concerned her parents. She had somersaulted backwards to some moment of nexus between them all which skewed the familial triangle first female-wise then male-wise in sharp differentiation. Janet Allotson could not have said how the memory was released, what night-pertaining mechanism might have set it free, but contemplated, in any case, in the quiet grey of dawn, in the blue chill of the hour (plus omnipresent traffic sounds, faint trills of thrush song, the slight movement of the body lodged deep sleeping beside her), the strange and involuntary grace of its recurrence.

The memory was dual. In the first part she watched her mother paint a picture in watercolours. It was her seventh year. She stood at the kitchen table and studied the movement of her mother's hand as it dipped and swirled a paintbrush, took up a flame-shape of colour, and then dispersed it on a page lambent and glistening with damp. She did not know what it was that the brush lines represented; it was an abstraction of forms principally scarlet and orange and meaningful, perhaps, by colour alone. The hand rose and dipped slowly in repeated parabolas, the forms swelled and gathered pigment, became more bloody and bright, began to extend unimpeded to the perimeters of the paper.

Two things were curious: the mother wore on that day a scarlet dress, and had also rouged her cheeks, a cosmetic indulgence usually reserved for special occasions. This repetition of colour, so neatly coincident, so oval on oval, implicated the woman mysteriously in her work; the girl-child Janet Allotson thought it odd and remarkable. She gazed at her mother's face, at her hair, at her dress, at the curve of her shape, at the rim of light along her body from the sunshine at the window, and noted the stillness and fixity with which she worked. Some magnification of vision attended this scrutiny. Janet saw fragments of golden wattle blossom caught in the hair, saw how the fabric of the dress described breasts and hips, noticed, glancing surreptitiously beneath the kitchen table, streaks of dirt on long bare feet, not unlike her own. The child observed her mother with unprecedented concentration, as though it was the first time ever she had seen her whole, a mother entire.

The painter continued apparently undistracted. Whorls and complex flourishes appeared beneath the brush. Gradations of shadow produced what might have been petals. There was a suggestion of figures or flesh, dunes in a desert landscape, blown water, a bowl of apples. Janet stood there at the table and contemplated with all her seven year old seriousness the page upon which images were both fluidly uncertain and wonderfully whim-dependent.

Then, quite unexpectedly, she heard herself pronounce, for the first time in her life and from who-knows-where, the story book word 'ruby'. It formulated itself in the chamber of her mouth, verged forward and was uttered: 'ruby'. A capacious word, cadenced, consonantal — oriental, somehow, and possibly Aladdinish, summoning tessellated window lattices, incense burners of brass filigree, tasselled velvet robes, anti-gravitational, speed-unlimited carpets, sunsets of pure peach over spiky minarets, dome on breast-shaped dome for mile after Middle Eastern mile. 'Ruby': this single word opened like a window upon an altogether-elsewhere.

Did her mother glance up? Was there some instant of understanding or complicity between them? Did the hand pause at its making or the form at its refinement? Janet Allotson could not remember. At the centre of her recollection — in some ways so redolent of child examination (detail, curiosity, the low-eye view) — rested a single dull naught, a mere forgetting of response. The word 'ruby' was indubitable, but after that came an interval of momentary amnesia, a flat-shaped nothing, a no-mother with a no-smile, a no-current of maternal inquiry and approbation. It was a 'ruby' unrequited.

(Janet thought now in terms of legal casuistry: *Quot non apparet non est*: 'That which does not appear does not exist'.)

At this point commences the second part of the memory. Janet's father appeared all of a sudden at the kitchen door. A large man of squarish frame and robust disposition, enormous hands, farmerish clothes (mud-caked, work-soiled, sweetly odour-laden), he stamped at the doorway to announce his entrance (a habit taken from his own father and conveyed onwards, gender indifferent, right down the generations) and flashed an open-bladed pocket knife before his daughter.

'The skinning', he reminded. 'Time for men's work.'

Janet turned from the painting and tucked the word ruby in the side of her cheek like a forbidden mouthful.

She dutifully followed her father to the lower paddock down by the creek. He dragged by the tail a grey kangaroo they had hit with the truck two days before. The sky was yellow and warm, the air placidly breezeless. At each intruding footstep insects sprang up in tiny clouds from the high grass. (Janet found this comical:

that one's progress might be signified by puffs abuzz.)

They reached the narrow creek and her father placed the dead animal on a patch of bald grass not far from the water. Janet squatted to look: it was the first skinning she had witnessed.

The kangaroo had wholly closed up with its death. Bounding life gone, it was now limp and shut-eyed, a pretty face indifferent and blank as a mask. Father turned it on its back so that the hind legs splayed apart and the short little forelegs jutted forward, pathetically, in a supplicating gesture. It appeared vaguely prayerful, as small pawed animals sometimes do, but Janet knew, even then, that a skinning must disqualify anthropomorphism or sentimentality.

She watched the insertion of the knife into the chest of the animal. It punctured and was drawn down the length of the carcass in a slightly jagged movement. Then came the separation of skin from flesh. The knife pushed gently under, and the skin with its fur was peeled carefully away. First of all the chest and the belly were exposed. Janet held her breath.

It was not, as she had imagined, the compact containment of the body that impressed her — the hill of bowed ribs and the tight bowl of belly — but a spectacle of colours. Beneath and adhering to the dingy grey fur was a layer of lime green fat, and beneath that, upon the body, pastels of every shade. Sinews stretched lines in streaks of lilac, there was the soft pink of flesh, blue traceries of blood, a yellow of some unidentifiable substance, and all glistened together as though covered with water or a thin sheet of plastic. Janet thought it most beautiful, a revelation. Instead of butcher incarnadine, this unexpected subtlety.

The knife worked away so that the skin of the kangaroo continued to draw back: more planes of colour, more tidy rotundity. The blade was inscribing a series of quick curves, flensing as it went. The father bent at his work, not once looking up, and slowly removed the pelt with all the unhurried fastidiousness of a waiter handling an expensive and tailor-precise dinner jacket.

But when the carcass was turned over to complete the procedure Janet experienced a slight moment of shock. On the flesh of the rump was a large blackened area which showed the damage of impact. It was ugly and distracting and indicated unseemly death. Caught beneath the skin was a congealed and darkened sac which must surely spill open.

Yet the father, still silent, manoeuvred his knife skilfully across this terrible territory. Janet wanted to close her eyes (oh the thud of that body, the too-new corpse of the kangaroo propelled, larrikin-like, over the momentous bonnet, the sure and simple finality of its quivering rest) but did not. She watched the skin come away, watched the knife wiped clean on threads of dry grass, watched as the carcass, now sullied and too old to be safely eaten, was dragged off into a patch of bushes for a private decomposition.

Janet's father rolled the kangaroo skin so that it formed a tight scroll.

'Your mother', he said. 'Take it to your mother.'

And he lay back on the grass, extracted a cigarette from behind his ear, and lit up.

There is no walk back to the house with the stinking skin, no return journey through insect puffs; this route has been cancelled, this journey unregistered. There is only a moment of resolution; or irresolution.

Janet was there at the doorway with her animal parcel (stamping her feet), and saw that her mother was still painting. The hand lifted and sank, dabbed precisely, lifted again and twirled with a slow whisk a lovely globe of colour. The painting was more elaborate, but still incomprehensible. Janet felt she wanted to speak. She wanted to say the word 'ruby' and so attract her mother's attention. She might reconstruct that moment of exotic vista, find again that point of aperture through which she glimpsed a locality that could only have been fiction. If there was any vision now attached it was indistinct, uncertain and caught, she supposed, behind a layer of pink membrane: there was some inkling of another existence both absolutely fantastic — lodged in phonology and imagination, in the sleepy inflections of a bedtime reading voice — and profoundly organic — intimate and substantive as the beating heart of one's body. There seemed, in that moment, an urgent need for reclamation.

But some obstruction was at work. Janet remained silent. She stood with her word unuttered and the skin unscrolled. It was a moment in which she felt — and such a premature revelation! — an appalling sensation of the disconnectedness of things: her father by the creek, her mother fixed at the painting, the exposed kangaroo, at once splendid and awful, the insects, the blossom, the sound of far cows moaning.

Janet looked at her mother, dropped the skin in the doorway, and, accelerated by an uncontrollable haywire of emotion, ran off through the grass to seek a secret crying place.

Janet Allotson, barrister, hugged a cover around her body and moved to the bay window. It was a blue Melbourne morning in which hung, as one would expect, a possibility of drizzle. Childhood was elsewhere, dry, golden coloured, and irreparably preterite. The bedroom had assumed an aspect of indeterminacy, in part a certain quality of the blurring early light, in part a consequence of her own groping through distant past selves and their distant past implications. It carried the exquisite tension of an inner chronology.

There was a case, Janet recalled, which she had been told of in her student days and which returned to her now as an extraordinary exemplar of the misery of forgetfulness. A strange young man, accused by the crown of the murder of his mother, had argued that he was simply unable to remember the incident. This was no casual absent-mindedness: according to the defence the man had one year before suffered a terrible head injury after which he possessed no reliable or substantive continuity of self. He could remember, it was attested, only within a span of seven or eight days. Beyond that all was black. The mother, in fact, was entirely forgotten. Photographs of past life were entirely unrecognisable. And the man was thus condemned — as a neurologist witness for the defence sought to argue — to a perpetual selfhood merely one week old.

The only legal grounds employed fell within the plea of insanity, within a version, that is, of *non compos mentis.* The mental state was such that the man's faculties were adjudged not actually attenuated, but simply incomplete. Thus the accused, it was conceded, was not without emotions; but these were riddling, chaotic and unattached to the world. Nor was he lacking in the employment of language; however words too bore a manifest lack of attachment, a frailty, a flimsiness, an inconsequentiality. For all this the accused was a rational man, moderate and articulate. He was also evidently anguished at the thought that he might have killed his unmemorable mother. His own oblivion tortured him.

But there came a particular moment at which the case was clearly lost. Addressing the perplexed jury, counsel for the defence drew attention to a poignant anomaly in the accused's condition. Before his sad accident the man had been a student writing a thesis on Shakespeare's sonnets. And within the general realm of this man's forgetting, there existed a single and altogether striking exemption: he could recite, by heart, the complete sonnets of Shakespeare. As eloquent testimony — and not without a sense of courtroom flair — the lawyer requested that his client pronounce sonnet number thirty:

When to the sessions of sweet silent thought
I summon up remembrance of things past,
I sigh the lack of many a thing I sought,
And with old woes new wail my dear times' waste:...

At this point the jury replaced perplexity with scepticism. No reciter of Shakespeare could be claimed deficient in memory!: the defence lawyer had committed a ruinous error of judgement. The accused, in turn, was sentenced to life imprisonment, though an appeal saw him later placed in protective custody, for an indefinite term and at the Governor's pleasure, in the local lunatic asylum.

Within a week he had forgotten the outside world, and continued to live on in the inside world, within a system, exactly composed, of one hundred and fifty-four utterly discrete and elegant fourteen line universes, within, that is, a world almost entirely linguistic.

Janet Allotson shivered and moved back into bed. Her lover still slept. She slid her shape along his and rubbed her hand along his thighs. Then, without exactly knowing the reason why, though hoping to arouse, hoping to inspire a sleepily amorous response, hoping for a kiss and a reciprocating hand, a caress definitive, she bent over her lover's ear, leant her lips so close that they brushed its tip, and whispered, very seductively, the single word 'ruby'.

'Life Probably Saved by Imbecile Dwarf'

(Index entry in Ronald W. Clarke's Freud: The Man and the Cause, *Granada, 1982, for which exists only one slim and secretive paragraph of exposition.)*

Is the tape recorder on? Well, let me see.

It was a long time ago now of course. Vienna was still very lovely in those days, before so many cars filled up the streets with their noise and their roars, like great metal predators. There were more trees along the boulevard, the Ringstrasse. It was quieter, too, and the light was clean and more clear. Women were more beautiful, hats, red lips, men more polite, still bowing and with gloves.

I was only a junior nurse when Dr Deutsch admitted him, but I remember it well. It was some time in April, 1923. I remember the exact month because it was the very same month in which my Claus proposed marriage; I was in love, you see. Well one day in April Dr Deutsch brought in his patient Dr Freud for a biopsy. (We didn't know at that stage that he had cancer of the jaw; it seemed more likely to be benign, what we call a leukoplakia: smokers get them all the time.) One of the other nurses, I recall, came over to me and whispered, 'It is that sex doctor Freud; I'll bet he has contracted a cancer for his sins', and she squinted her eyes and looked maliciously in his direction. I shall never forget it. Greta, her name was. For myself I was surprised at how solid and how forceful he actually appeared. He was almost sixty-seven, and you think to yourself: sixty-seven, maybe cancer: frail, shrivelled. But he was not like that at all. Those photographs you showed me — where he looks at the camera directly and rudely, so like a man — that is more like it. He was elegantly dressed, carried a cane, wore a hat, had a neatly trimmed white beard above a black satin tie, oh, and a watch chain, as was the fashion those days, hanging from his waistcoat. Gold rings on his fingers. All very bourgeois. And, would you believe it, he came to the hospital smoking a cigar like a chimney! Ach! So stupid!

Dr Freud was supposed to be admitted for a quick biopsy and then taken home. He had an appointment with Dr Hajek, a rhinologist — a nose doctor, would you believe — in the outpatient clinic. So we hadn't booked him a bed, thinking there was no need. Not foreseeable, anyway. But then later Dr Hajek came striding up the corridor towards me and said in a loud voice (he was a very loud man) 'My patient Dr Freud has lost more blood than expected. We will leave him here overnight for observation. Arrange a bed if you please.' Well, can you imagine? Arranging beds wasn't my task but I fixed it up anyway, them being men of such importance, me being young and looking up to such men. (And not knowing then the sort of things I know now.)

You said this new biography will have lots of bits and pieces that the others left out — what did you call it? — 'marginalia based'. Well let me just tell you something really good. Dr Freud had a thing, a strange thing, about numbers, a superstition, a dread. You knew that already? Ach, never mind. Anyway, with some trouble I had found him a bed in ward five, but he straightaway objected. 'Wrong number', he mumbled with his hand up to his jaw. 'Wrong number.' He shook his head at me stern-like. I could see he was in pain and the bandages around his face were already soaking crimson, so I tried to be kind and settle the matter quickly. I took Dr Freud by the arm and led him to the tiny utility room, out towards the back, where we kept the dwarf. It was a room, incidentally — I remember it now — where there remained on the wall a portrait of the late emperor, Emperor Franz Josef. You used to see them everywhere in the days of my youth, in banks, in post offices, our Emperor with fluffy sideburns, but on his death in 1916 they all suddenly disappeared. But someone had retained just this single one, and hung it up regardless. It made you feel you had slipped a little backwards in time — with the old Emperor looking on, alive as ever in his picture. Anyway the room — numberless, as it happened — had only two cots and was very stuffy and dark, and not really fitted out for taking patients at all. But then the dwarf was an idiot, and didn't seem to notice. I helped Dr Freud onto the cot and then I said to Jacob — that's the dwarf — I said 'Jacob, this man is important. He is a doctor. He is good. You look after him, Jacob.'

Let me tell you about Jacob. He was just over one metre tall and very fat for his size, in addition, that is, to being an idiot. Every now and then, when he was sick (which was often) we had him in at the hospital, staying in the utility room. We didn't put him in a ward because he tended to disturb all the other patients with his songs. Always singing was Jacob. Usually it was lullabies, but rather disjointed and hard to follow, if you know what I mean. I think he made them up. All moonlight and mothers, sometimes bits of Yiddish. Starry nights, soft winds, that sort of thing. A bit of humming, too.

Jacob — this will surprise you — had both a mother and a wife. We think of these people as alone somehow, don't we? But Jacob lived with his small family in an apartment only two doors away from my rooms: that was how I knew. His mother was a tall and willowy woman, about forty, I think. She looked like a silent movie star, very dark and pale, a lovely face with definite lips of the sort that men of my generation go for: tightly pursed, pointed, and in the shape of a heart. Grey eyes — beautiful — a remote and rather nowhere-looking gaze. Anyway, I only spoke to her once or twice, so I can't really say we were actually acquainted. But I saw her a lot, standing at the window of her apartment that fronted the street, looking straight out. She would just stand there and stare. Sometimes men paused or slowed down as they walked past, but she never seemed to notice them. She just stood looking out. Sort of desolate and thoughtful.

The daughter-in-law, I must say, was much more interesting: you must put her in your book. Bertha, her name was. She was an idiot, too. I often wondered how they got together, Jacob and Bertha, how they managed to find each other at all in such a large city, and avoid the institutions. Anyway, Bertha was normal sized but had, poor woman, the strangest condition. She had some kind of facial palsy that fixed her face rather awkwardly in a permanent smile. It was quite disconcerting. Her head hung down to one side, and her mouth tilted upwards. I remember I first met her on my way to the subway on Karlsplatz — I was meeting my Claus after work and we were going off together to have tea with his mother. I saw, from a distance, that a man was accosting her. He was proposing obscenities and she had her face turned away from him, sad and smiling. Her cheeks were very red and her eyes brimmed with tears, but the contradicting smile must have given this fellow the wrong message. He had his hand on her breast, and there she was smiling. I rushed up to the man and struck him with my carry-bag. 'How dare you!' I said. 'How dare you take advantage!' (I was very confident for my age.) Bertha immediately recognised me as some kind of neighbour, stepped forward and clutched my arm. So I was hitting with one side and had the idiot on the other. The man immediately withdrew. Seeing my nurse's uniform perhaps he thought me an authority of some kind. Anyway, he withdrew. I took Bertha by the hand and delivered her home, forgetting entirely about my meeting with Claus and the appointment with his mother. (Later I remembered, and had to write a note of apology, on pretty coloured paper, as was the custom in those days. Mind you, it did Claus no harm at all to be left waiting and expectant.)

I actually saw Bertha quite often after that. Believe it or not we became good friends. Sometimes on Sundays we would walk down to the park together, arm in arm. On the Sundays, that is, that Jacob was in hospital. I can't for the life of me imagine what we talked about — Bertha being as she was, though not as dim as you might expect — but I recall that our short times together were pleasant. Apart from Claus, who, as a working man, worked very long hours, I didn't really know many people in the city. (My family, you see, were all back in Eisenerz.) So I enjoyed her company. When Jacob came home from the hospital we sometimes, all three, went out walking together — but not very often. I didn't mind being seen in the company of Bertha, but with the two of them together we were really very conspicuous, and attracted attention. Once in the park a little girl screamed and burst into tears when she saw us coming, all three, along the path towards her. A terrible thing. A real sweetie, too.

I forgot to mention, by the way, that Bertha was employed. Well, part-time, in fact. She was employed doing menial chores two days a week at the home of Karl Kraus — you may have heard of him — the notorious writer of nasty pamphlets. The story goes that Karl Kraus had been out walking one day — no doubt on the lookout for scandals to print and embarrass — and spied our dear Bertha. Interested, for some reason, he followed her home where he proposed to the mother a contract of employment. I have no idea — it seems so rash and irresponsible — why she accepted. They did not appear hard up, but then you never can be sure with other people, can you? And to such a man!

One day the mother came to me — it was already evening (the lamps were on) and I was just home from work — and asked me if I would go and fetch Bertha from Herr Kraus's house. It seems she was late, much, much later than usual. Why the mother didn't go herself I really don't know, though now that I think about it she hardly ever went out. Anyway, it was the very first time she had come to my rooms, and as she was a commanding and mysterious woman, I felt it must be important and so agreed to the errand. The mother handed me a piece of paper with the address printed on it in a perfectly neat hand, and I set out through the dark.

Can you imagine? I was asked to wait in the parlour while a woman went to fetch her. Very fancy it was; very bourgeois. Long mirrors, Turkish rugs, silk coverings on the furniture, two columns in the doorway with identical candlesticks, stiff chairs, Venetian glass. Before the woman returned, there was Karl Kraus himself — much kinder looking than I had imagined, and rather vulnerable, I think, behind those rimless glasses — leading Bertha by the hand and bringing her forward. He said something like: 'So you have come to fetch Bertha, Bertha the very symbol of Vienna herself: beguiling grin on the outside, crescent, conventional, covering like a mask the imbecile vacancy within'. Just like that! Those very words! And he said this, mind you, in such a friendly tone that for a moment I was not sure at all how to respond. But then I realised what he had said, how unpleasant, how uncalled for, and seized Bertha from him, turned swiftly and left, without uttering in reply a single word. Such an awful man! I shall never forget it.

But I have digressed, haven't I? It is the Freud story, isn't it, you wish to know.

Dr Freud was placed, as I said, in the utility room with Franz Josef and the idiot dwarf Jacob. He seemed settled when I left him, and I assumed he would sleep. I went on with other duties nearby, just up the corridor, and to be honest quite forgot that he was with us. But then, to my astonishment, there was Jacob running towards me in his clumsy fat-man way and shouting at the top of his head: 'The blood of doctor! The blood of doctor!' I shall never forget it. I rushed back to the room — with Jacob stumbling at my heels — to see Dr Freud lying prostrate in a mess of new blood. The bandages on his face were completely soaked, and his hands were bloody also, as though he had tried to stop the flow by clasping them to his wound. And the whole of his pillow was red and damp, a profuse haemorrhage, in short, and still streaming out. I felt suddenly guilty — knowing this man's importance, knowing he was stuck here in the utility room with the dwarf, knowing that a doctor would have to be immediately found. I settled Jacob by the bed to watch over Dr Freud, and hurried off for a physician. What a wasted effort! Dr Hajek was nowhere at all to be found; he had left after surgery. So I rushed back to the utility room without a doctor. The dwarf Jacob, thank God, was still in attendance. With one hand he held the dangling hand of poor Sigmund Freud, the other he had firmly fastened at Dr Freud's jaw, perhaps in imitation of something he had seen earlier. It was a curious sight, and might have looked, at a glance, as though Jacob had just committed some shocking crime, and was busy hushing up the screams of his victim. But in fact he was tender and firm and gentle as a child. More sensible, too, than I'd had reason to believe.

I pushed him aside and set about repair work. Pressure. New bandages. Binding. More pressure. (Until the doctor came and took over — as doctors do.) I learned later that our patient had been very close to death, and that the dwarf had certainly saved him by raising the alarm and helping to stop the blood. (No thanks to Dr Hajek who should have stuck to noses.)

When the crisis was over the patient communicated on paper — since he could now not speak at all without extreme discomfort — that he would like to remain in the utility room rather than move to a ward. This surprised us all, especially in the light of his later accusations. (You will know, of course, that Dr Freud later charged that the hospital had been deliberately negligent since its staff was jealous and resentful of the success of psychoanalysis!) Anyway, he stayed, recuperating for a few days where he had first been put. His daughter Anna slept on a chair in the same awful room.

There is something — let me tell you — I have always remembered. Bertha came to visit while Dr Freud was still there. She didn't often visit Jacob when he was stuck there in hospital; for some reason I think — though I'm not sure why — that the mother prohibited it. Still she came in one day, and this is how I see them. Dr Freud is propped up in bed with a heavily bandaged jaw, with the face of Emperor Franz Josef hovering alive above his head. In comes our dear Bertha — I led her in myself — who goes straight over to Jacob and gives him one of those cumbersome and slobbering embraces that such people seem invariably to have. Quite touching, really. Kisses, holding hands. Dr Freud had been observing her and beckoned with his finger for Bertha to come over to him. Which she did, smiling. Then he held her face in both hands and ran his fingers carefully over her features as though he were somehow medically appraising her odd condition. (The smile, I mean, not the idiocy.) A sort of medical appraisal. I watched him very closely and thought for just one moment, just one moment, mind you, that he was going to cry. He didn't, of course; men didn't in those days. But just for one moment I thought that he would. The famous Sigmund Freud crying; can you imagine?

No, I know nothing more of the idiot dwarf Jacob; I'm sorry to say. Except that he died of complications of pneumonia not very long after, early, I think it was, in 1924. Bertha and the mother stayed on in the apartment, though I moved out to live with my husband Claus. I heard later that they were taken away by the Nazis — two of the first to go, and her no longer by that time looking like a silent movie star with heart shaped lips, but much, much older, and her hair gone grey as her eyes. No one seems to know of their final fate, but one can guess, of course, where Nazis are concerned.

Really, there is nothing more I can tell you about Jacob. I know you want to write up the dwarf part of the story but I remember other things. When I think back on Jacob and the time of the biopsy, I think mostly of the women. I think of the mother at her window, so beautiful and quiet, and most of all of dear Bertha, who was always smiling and affectionate, and a friend despite all. And whom that terrible man — Karl Kraus was his name — said one night was somehow the very symbol of Vienna.

Veronica

My colleague said of this story: it is a Veronica myth; there is nothing more to it. A dismissive sneer arose on his face, scholastic, stringent and unimpeachably sure.

This story begins where it should, at a point of arrival. The place of its initial action is a North Indian railway station, a largish rural town, a hot mid-summer. There is the predictable Asian plenitude, a cram of human bodies impossibly compressed, too many people inhabiting too tiny a space. In the rush for exits some will fall under, a child will be lost, a parcel mislaid, a sari ripped, a precious fragment of food dropped to the ground and crushed underfoot. There are all the complex versions of random and purposive movements that constitute the rude democracy of crowds. The noise of the place adds another plenitude, since every area is loud. Greetings and anxious exclamations over luggage mingle with the reprimand of children, shouts of hawkers and the squeaks and clangs of exhausted machinery. And superintending all, like a deific manifestation in this land of many deities, are booming messages issuing incessantly from a public address system corrupted by static.

Our heroine Elizabeth makes her way tourist-eager through the interstices of the crowd. She has a certain bravura, a certain intentness of purpose. Against the mass of milling people she defines herself singular and somewhat elect. Let us say she has also the smugness of a conqueror: having governed her unease at bodies and smells, at the different skins of others, she wishes now to repose in first world sovereignty, to enjoy what she sees for its souvenirs and its spectacles. She moves with confidence, clutching at her travel pack in tenacious regard for the hands of thieves. She easily defies the jostling abrasions of the crowd, at first elbowing through groups decomposing before her, then sidling apologetically or stretching in a leap to straddle a gutter. At her back lies a stench she has not yet accommodated: the particular pungency of hot metal machinery. It is something of her own world, something, perhaps, reminiscent of accidents. She discounts this distraction and moves quickly away.

Our heroine Elizabeth moves away towards odours which will later summon India more suddenly and immitigably than any of the photographs she pauses daily to capture. The scent of samosas turning in oil. The alliterative ingredients of cardamom, chilli, cumin, coriander. The perfume of saffron. The sourdough of chapatis. Some unpronounceable coconut condiment which dampens down curry. Curd. Vindaloo. She inhales deeply and indulgently and then proceeds to order, with all the opulent indifference of a millionaire, whatever takes her fancy. The seller squats on the floor in dirty robes. He is dextrous in servitude. He presents a plate of torn cardboard and piles it neatly and efficiently with a serve of food which is spare but impressively redolent; and Elizabeth stuffs down her meal with unseemly haste, aware of no censure.

Enough money brought our heroine to what the urchin guide falsely claimed was the best hotel in town. It was tolerably shabby and called, in its much smaller English translation, the Lux. Framing the name were a pair of reversed swastikas, a symbol Elizabeth had at first, and ingenuously, misunderstood as fascistic. Now knowing better (from the Sanskrit *svastika,* from *svasti:* well being, fortune, luck), she smiles to herself wisely (with the wisdom of guidebooks), and decides that the Lux is sufficient for one night.

The hotel room, however, has a quality of chastening decrepitude. The bed is of wooden slats, has but the slightest shred of mattress, and bears a coverlet marked all over with stains of semen and urine. There is no other furniture, not even a chair. In one corner of the room stands an earthenware jug of water, a modest touch remarkable only for its presence.

Elizabeth considers the embarrassment of asking for her money back, of seeking out a new urchin and traipsing back through the streets, but resolves to stay — for one night only — where circumstance has placed her.

The room has one feature not yet described: there is a large double window that commands an excellent view of the busy street below. So while inside is all vacancy and a smear of past lives, outside, just through the window, is a present tense full of people and noisy activity only marginally less crowded than the clamorous railway station.

Elizabeth positions herself on the narrow sill of this window and considers the scene. Containing little to photograph, it is judged uninteresting. Workers work, sellers sell, shoppers buy. There are bicycles and bullock carts. Motorised minicabs. An occasional car. A woman in an emerald sari is flirting with a young man who has papers under his arm. To the left an older woman weeps alone in a shadow. There is a scatter of escaped chickens and a man with a stick. Another woman, also old, roasts peanuts over a burner and sells them in little cones made from discarded newspapers. Children who ought to be in school chase about, dashing bright colours. And overall hangs suspended a fine white dust, one set moving in the air with each active intervention as though registering ethereally lives otherwise terrestrial, caught and solid. It is this dust Elizabeth pauses momentarily to ponder. She suspects it pestilential, and will stay just one night.

The afternoon seems interminable. An excursion outside to spend money and take photographs is futile and demoralising. The town, as it happens, is ill appointed for tourists seeking solace and diversion. Elizabeth retreats to her room and rejecting the bed — which offends the hotel obligation to obliterate precession and present each room anew — lays her sleeping bag on the floor and reclines into hardness.

She takes from her worn travel pack a paperback book,

Thomas Mann's *The Magic Mountain*. It had been discarded much earlier as too Germanic for her taste, too cumbersome and earnest, but in the circumstances she is prepared to tackle it once more. Elizabeth opens the pages of her portable Europe, and displaces, word by word, the shabby room, the inhospitable town, the suspect, grey, circumambient dust, with the grandiloquence and august gravity of the Alps. She enters mountains and cold air. Cultivated voices debate the verities. Sensibilities quiver. Clouds are uplifting. Ice, snow. The text possesses some aspect of lyrical refinement that, existing only in fictive places for which no passport is required, is both immediately soothing and automatically accommodating: *From the rugged slopes came the sound of cowbells; the peaceful, simple, melodious tintinnabulation came floating unbroken through the quiet, thin, empty air, enhancing the mood of solemnity that broods over the valley heights.*

At twilight something noisy is happening outside. Through the window and the darkening air comes the sound of voices growing louder and music swelling at a distance. Elizabeth rises from her sleeping bag, flings the Alps dismissively, and moves to the window. Something is happening a little further up the street: a procession is approaching. She seizes her camera and scampers downstairs to witness whatever it is.

Crowds of people stand back against the rows of buildings. Ahead through the dust, now agitated, dense and sinuously spiralled, is an advancing wedding party. The honoured couple sit high on a bullock cart bedecked with dozens of garlands of orange and yellow marigolds. Above them is a canopy of some unusual silver fabric: it shines in the half light — doubly for a row of bright coins that sway and tinkle at its luxurious fringe. The couple, who stare stiffly ahead giving no sign of affection, also wear money. The man has a jacket festooned with rupee notes; the bride has more notes fluttering loosely in her lap. She is additionally weighted with jewellery of gold, a ring through her nose, heavy chains at the throat and the temple, a large pair of expensive ear-rings finely wrought. They are, in short, a dazzling pair, felicitously translated into the idol-like pose of the nation's archetypes. Statue still they fix, albeit gaudy with wealth, fertility itself: blooms, riches, beneficence, light. (Our heroine adjusts her camera lens to fix the couple further.)

At each side of the bullock cart, walking in single file, a train of people carry bamboo poles mounted with electric lights. This seems to Elizabeth odd and incongruous. Her tourist soul would have preferred the enveloping soft focus of lanterns or candles. Moreover it sets a trail of ugly black cords streaming backwards from the procession, giving the appearance that the whole event is somehow run by electricity, that it is an artificial energy that moves and articulates the splendour of the party. Musicians in attendance contribute to this sense: they weave through the light bearers with a mechanical jerkiness. Only children seem exempt and with characteristic anarchy act in dissident form, running about in their best clothes, flinging rose petals indecorously from baskets and bowls. The petals fall slowly, buoyed on warm air; the dust, in contradistinction, swirls upwards to the heavens in speedy dispersal.

For some moments Elizabeth is almost unaware that a new sound is approaching. Her face is in the camera; she is concentrated on the visual. But then, noting discordancy, she recovers her eyes and looks to see what it is. At some distance from the cart, coming up from behind, are two men carrying an electric generator between them on a platform. The long black cords converge to where they are; they are the source of the light.

What is terrible is that the men are so obviously beggars. Their dereliction is extreme. The man closest to Elizabeth is filthy, emaciated and almost naked; the one on the other side is little better off. Elizabeth feels rather offended at this terrible bad taste: to situate so proximate the gorgeous and the miserable. She lowers her camera and feels an illness arise within her. The noise of the generator is huge and rasping. There is a smell of hot metal.

What happens occurs quickly. Tourist and beggar exchange short, swift glances; they meet, as it were, within the transit of a gaze. Then the beggar slips away. He stumbles in his path and begins falling into the crowd, falling much more heavily than his frail and disappearing shape would ever seem to suggest. Instinctually aroused, Elizabeth rushes to catch him. At this precise moment the generator loosens and slides on to her, halting upon the arm she had extended as support. Her flesh begins to sear. Metal burns away a disfiguring impression. The pain is exact: Elizabeth has never before felt so definite and empirical.

At this point my colleague proposes his scholarly explanation. According to late Mediaeval legend — the story is not Biblical — a woman of Jerusalem, stricken with great piety on witnessing Christ labouring with his cross on the way up to Calvary, seized off her head cloth, moved forward from the crowd, and handed it over. Christ wiped his tired brow and returned the cloth to the woman; whereupon it was found that the fabric bore a perfect, clear likeness of the Divine face. This image was to be called the Vera-Icon (true likeness); the woman in question became St Veronica. Your Elizabeth, he said, merely re-enacts. She becomes anonymous and cultural; she has no significance other than that she recycles with predictability a plot already orthodox, conventional and known. That the icon of suffering is transferred to the body is of no particular interest; she still exists as translation. Unoriginal, old.

As she collapses into the dust Elizabeth glimpses, with inexplicable clarity, the seller of peanuts. She sees a hand with paper cones and feels herself descend dizzily into a cone of her own.

Someone has clasped her. A man has her by the waist and lifts her up and away. She is aware of caramel-coloured arms encircling her like a lover. The man is speaking in Hindi. He is assuming control. The wedding has moved on, taking its noise and lights and hot burning metal; and now Elizabeth, perversely novel and with the extra attraction of serious injury, has become the new spectacle. She sees a dense curve of people move their semicircle before her. They are a terrible congregation. Choosing pain from the cone she chooses the latter, and slants and slides away into its tiny black end.

When Elizabeth awakens she is lying on her bed in the Hotel Lux. The rescuer is there with her, proclaiming in strange English that a doctor has been sent for. He bends down and casually takes up Thomas Mann's *The Magic Mountain*. He squats in the centre of the floor and having, apparently, nothing better to do, enters the Alps.

An hour or so passes and no doctor comes. The man leaves without a word, taking Thomas Mann with him. Elizabeth chooses to curl up once more inside the cone.

In the long day that follows she will turn and toss, thirst terribly for water, and replay again and again the vision that led to her accident. She will see money and lights and indecorous children. She will snap once again at the photographic images she had hoped to display. In a moment of lucidity it occurs to her that her camera has somewhere gone missing and she weeps at its loss as the blind might for sight; she feels not robbed but rather darkened and incapacitated.

Accepting the man at his word Elizabeth waits for the doctor. She lays back like a patient expecting at any moment care and commiseration, the salve of kind hands, the cleanliness of hospitals, medicinal somnolence. Nobody comes.

The day moves on without her, carrying sunlight from the large window in a slow, fluent slide down the facing wall, playing sounds from the street to prove that action continues, sending, from time to time, little clouds of grey dust to spiral and stir and settle down gradually, a shower of motes, in this tomb of a room.

Towards twilight Elizabeth rises from her bed to fetch water. She finds it impossible to lift the earthenware pot with one hand, and is forced to employ her good hand as a kind of primitive cup and lap from it like a dog. She lurches back to her bed, suddenly, surprisingly, with enough energy left to curse.

When the man arrives at night — turning on the light she had not bothered to deal with — the curses continue. Elizabeth is shocked at the strength of her abuse. If she could she would poison this unhelpful man with the very pain that had so ignominiously rendered her thus: maddened, prostrate, embracing a cone. The man advances swiftly and places his hand over her mouth.

Veronica, said my colleague, is additionally the name of the most classic cape movement of the Spanish bullfight. The cape is swung so slowly before the face of the charging bull that it resembles, so it is said, St Veronica's wiping of the Divine face. A gesture once holy becomes a signal of doom.

The man has one hand tightly over her cursing mouth and with the other is fumbling at the zip of her jeans. He exposes her thighs and is suddenly upon her, jerking back and forth like an electrical machine. Elizabeth sees the nameless face bobbing rhythmically above, its eyes tightly closed. She feels the pounding of a second pain on this bed more despicable with each passing moment. And then she remembers, as though the very page were still open before her: *From the rugged slopes came the sound of cowbells; the peaceful, simple, melodious tintinnabulation came floating unbroken through the quiet, thin, empty air, enhancing the mood of solemnity that broods over the valley heights.*

In the morning our heroine awakens sticky and bruised. Her arm is swollen and festered; she finds the sight of it repulsive. It rests like a dead thing on the stained coverlet.

Light and dust continue their floating migrations. Elizabeth is alone. She lays placidly listening to the many and various noises, intermittent and continual, human and inhuman, busy and tribal, that drift and enter from outside the window. With no view she re-creates the scene below: she hears a voice she imagines belongs to the woman with the emerald sari, she hears, or thinks she hears, that the older woman is still crying. There is a clatter of knocked pots and a rumble of bullock carts. Minicabs in acceleration. Chickens. Shouts. Religious chimes.

By afternoon this scene of sounds is so full and reverberative that seeing itself could lend no further corroboration that would make it more real. Thus Elizabeth is changed. Her skin has become caramel, her clothing a sari. She has felt her features remould: a longer nose with a jewel, broader lips, darker eyes, a gloss of black hair. Her body feels irreducibly local and exact; it correlates to its place, is attentive, identified.

My colleague says with authority: Elizabeth is unoriginal, a cipher, a blank, a mere structure of narrative. But I see her there lying upon the bed, lying just below the duplicitous swastika, substantial, abject, imagining the real, sending her mind up and about like a wisp of whirling dust, becoming explorative, becoming other, almost becoming, one might even say — with all the fraught politics of race in attendant complication — almost becoming Indian.

Babies

My sister, the lunatic, beckoned from the back shed with a tightly curled finger.

See the suns! she whispered. Come and see the suns!

She had a hucksterish tone that recalled the Easter fair. I remembered men with porous faces and leather money bags who leant repellently close and gestured backwards to bright stalls full of darts games or clown heads or soft furry toys.

No, I would say firmly, as girl-firm as possible. No.

My sister, the lunatic, was huckster insistent. She had hooked me with her finger, conspiratorially shrewd.

Come now, she said. Come and see all the suns.

Fractionally afraid, hesitant, nervous, I slid slowly forward into the shed's deep blue shadow, slid into position beside her bedraggled presence, her face the colour of contusions, her insuperable will, and answered in a single word: Yes!

It was five years ago that Rose became as she is. During her pregnancy — she was then sixteen and I a mere twelve — she began hearing voices that struggled upwards from her womb and entered volubly and invasively through the back of her head. In those days her face was rather chalk-coloured and gaunt and she carried on her brow the premature curve of a frown, as though acknowledging to the world the authority and the burden of her private chamber of words. She held one-sided conversations and replied to silent questions. She addressed invisible entities in slick polemics. She cajoled and persuaded. She waxed confidently lyrical. She debated, dictated, declaimed and discoursed. Whole dictionaries gathered in her small oval mouth. Dozens of alphabets were daily accomplished. With no skerrick of concision she entered a madwoman's realm of perpetual, involutional, loud-mouthed pronouncement.

I remember her sitting for long hours beneath the shade of our trellised grapevine. She was sturdy and still as a monument of granite. Leaf shapes quivered at her pallid face, or slid across the slopes of her bulbous body. And from the animate mouth: word upon word upon word upon word, grape clustered and almost innumerable.

There were also, of course, certain intervals of silence, certain long autistic stillnesses during which, I presume, Rose listened to her womb words. In these pauses she cocked her head somewhat oddly and distractedly at an angle which implied that the voices were very quiet and that she must strain hard to listen. I wondered as I watched — my appalled fascination growing faster than her belly — whether by an act of will I might also hear the voices that commanded of my sister such strict attention. I began to long for her sounds; I began to covet her correspondents; I began to wish also — lying silent in the dark, listening to her babble bounce out through the night, listening to verbs, adjectives, a whole world full of nouns, tumble, tongue-untied, in wonderful conjugations — I began to wish also for a womb full of words. My jealousy was unspeakable. I lay in my bed feeling ordinary and stupid. I was thin and wordless, unpregnant, plain.

Then, at last, in the white enamel of moonlight, in the velvet air still invisibly hung with the echoes of her words, she would become exhausted. Rose would turn very slowly the enormous bauble of her body, cease her loud babble, and finally sleep.

My mother beckoned from her bedroom with a crooked finger. I remember it well.

Your sister is a lunatic, she firmly pronounced. Unhinged. Unstable. In a state of excess.

And with those words she turned and led me into her bedroom, a territory usually denied us and thus filled with the sharp specialness of prohibition. To be admitted to my mother's room was a sign of particular gravity; I knew it only from doorway glimpses, apart from the single occasion — just after my father died — when I was allowed into its centre and almost choked on the concentration of maternal essences: powderscent, knick-knacks, a violet wallpaper grotesquely floral, suffocating dust, flimsy lace curtains, squat china statues, faceted glass bottles, body odours, trinkets, charms of every kind. And beyond all that, altar-like in its presence and wholly commanding, stood an oak dressing-table surmounted in style by a bright three planed mirror which caught and triplicated every girlish trepidation. I had itemised this room through constant recollection and followed my mother inwards to confirm or disconfirm a memory much too vivid to approximate the real. Strangulating tendrils still hung upon the wall, there was still a density of air, a multiplicity of objects, but the whole appeared, over all, rather domestic and subdued, less strange and disturbing than my practised vision. Only the oak dressing-table with its surveilling mirror — a piece of furniture of corpulent and almost Buddhic dimensions — retained any of the original, time-tested power. It sat in the corner with imposing amplitude; I found it fearful.

My mother moved to the mirror and became suddenly three.

Sit beside me, she said, patting the narrow vanity stool. I stepped forward to join the company of mothers and daughters, thinking to myself all the while: I am here in her room, she has let me right in, it is less fearful, less large, less an organic entrapment, but there is this triptych of selves, these lustrous faces, this mysterious confrontation. I eyed myself shyly. Each angle showed me timid and unimportant; my mother's face, by comparison, was impressive and florid and firmly in existence. (I thought of Rose beneath the grape leaves or turning in the moonlight, less a face now than a voluptuous noisy bud of a body.)

You must not, she began, you must not listen, on any account, to your lunatic sister. Pay no attention, ignore her, walk right away. She is unhinged and unstable. Disturbed. Deranged.

My mother looked straight ahead and glanced at my image; I thought her quick gaze exceptionally imperious and severe. The glass of the mirror held me still for inspection; I was ensnared and detained in its silver series of verticals. There then ensued a moment of complete, static silence. My mother's lovely white hands fiddled unconsciously and fastidiously with objects disposed about the dressing-table, a hair brush, a crystal ring case, the edge of a crocheted doily, and then came delicately to rest on a jewellery box of teak inlaid with slivers of ivory.

I have, she began again, a proposition to make.

My mother opened the teak box and drew out her jewels. (Ah, the perfection of her fingers! The authority of her gaze arrowing, tangentially, straight for mine!)

This is a brooch given me by your father in our wedding year. (She held a cluster of tiger eyes set in figured silver.) And this is a necklace which belonged to my dead sister Lily after whom, as you know, you are named in remembrance. (She raised a string of oval garnets, let them dangle and sway.) This here, you see, is my eternity ring (a band of rubies); this chain an heirloom from my maternal grandmother (an ugly cross spiked at the edges and complete with a crucified Jesus).

At this point I believe I must have ceased to wholly listen. Varieties of gold, corals, Chinese jade, Indian brass, linked swirls of silver, opal ear-rings alike: all were carried from the box and displayed singly and anecdotally. All summoned presences and ghosts, referred to former affections or lost infatuations, coffin-snaffled loves, family tree configurations. I had never before seen such treasure, nor been so much aware of the accoutrements of others.

And this, she said lastly, is the most special of all.

My mother raised a small ring of unidentifiable stones: it was a circle of blue gems, interspersed with tiny filigree patterned into leaves.

This was my own mother's. I will give it to you if you are still a virgin on your twenty-first birthday.

The ring was placed in my hand and I felt the sudden, uncomplicated vertigo of desire. It was an exquisite object. It would one day be mine. I glimpsed a fulfilment of expectations of solidity and immanence; I thought the attainment of the ring would place me surely in the net of family continuities, and would also guarantee — as though it were bridal — a definitive release from the realm of girlish inexperience.

Three mothers nodded in unison in the shiny glass as if reading in my thoughts a contract of souls.

The baby stayed for eight weeks. Rose kept it in our room, attending to its needs like a legitimate mother. She rose to it at night, changed nappies and suckled. She was calm and competent and moreover continued as garrulous as ever. No change in her condition of unusual fluency — as my mother predicted — had accompanied the birth. No cessation with parturition. No emptying or full-stop. No seizure of the larynx or tying of the tongue. Rose sat beneath the grapevine, now skeletal and stark against the autumn sky, bobbed her new baby in a sort of perpetual mobility, and continued prodigiously to speak.

As I recollect now there is little to relate. I took scarcely any interest in Rose's baby; it seemed merely to confirm her own exclusivity and my sad estrangement. She bent close above it, sought its vague stare, played with its tiny, pliable fingers, dressed and undressed its series of pastels, all with a kind of decentred fixation, as though the community of two was little different, in fact, to the community of one. I once attempted a fumbling aunt's embrace, more out of curiosity than genuine affection, only to be rebuffed by Rose's absolute refusal to acknowledge my presence. She simply talked past me, cancelled my brief gesture with a speech to an unseen addressee located somewhere in the space to my left.

I realise now that I did not comprehend my sister's speeches. Again and again came a torrent of articulate and sensational gibberish, words of such immediate and bodily power, such sensual investment, that I was giddy with the possibilities of a secret life I imagined Rose to have somehow, mother-defiant, accomplished. I thought for the first time of lovers and nakedness. I began, like her, to cherish the sounds of words, became, like her, a precocious word-hoarder. In puzzlement and enchantment I listened as she daily flung out mouthfuls of polysyllables, spoke on bodies, on babies, on the intricacies of sexual pleasure. And with young-sisterly deference, I acquiesced to her power.

Yet this was also something of a state of guilt and confusion.

With the birth Rose had recovered the specificity of her face; her body deflated, and I noticed once again the clear likeness between us. I noticed that we shared the same longish features, the same nut-brown eyes, the same fulsome mouth, the same abundant wayward hair. And this sameness was the basis for a terrible ambiguity: I both loved and feared my lunatic sister. She began to remind me of my mother's mirror, that there existed a realm of vision — cold, rational, utterly uncircumspect — within which too many of one's selves may pre-emptively appear.

Alone I worked to reconsolidate singularity. I remembered the ring of unusual blue stones, its lapidary definitiveness. The inanimate solidity of objects attracted me. Their neutral realm. Their uncarnal equipoise. Their complete autonomy.

It was not until early this year that I made a discovery: I discovered the existence of a hidden stack of audio-tapes. Without our knowledge mother had furtively recorded hours and hours of Rose's monologues in order to use them, eventually, as evidence in her committal. I waited until my mother had left the house, seized the tapes, all labelled 'Rose', and as though somehow releasing her imprisoned spirit, played each right through, from beginning to end. With a tight pang of misery I heard my sister's lovely voice, floating now disembodied and faceless through the years.

It emerges finished and unfinished. It is nothing human. The body it wears is illfitting and discoloured, the face ancient and anonymous. Eyes are not immediately round or apparent, hair is dispersed spirally, teeth not at all. The hands are inclined to Egyptianly scroll or flex open communicative, the most expressive of accessories. There is a softish skull, congenitally bubble-like — God-blown for the fun of it — and disproportionately achieved.

It is a system of contradictions. There are eruptive quakings, disarticulate limbs, and then, conversely, tiny quiet quivers and a suspended repose of mysterious integrity. The first is a flailing executed unharmonious; the second a recovery of almost spherical solidity within which, apparently, completion occurs. Unfinished awake, in sleep it closes off circuits, is sufficient, efficient, a neat functioning whole. (Above whom the Madonna checks to detect breathing.)

Its repetitions are astounding. Too openly orificed it issues loud, petulant and toothless notes from a face mostly mouth and the deepest of crimsons. Audible everywhere its hullabaloo insubordinate, its emissions unignorable and contrived upon the nerves. Other ended is the site of another recurrence: assiduous, copious, altogether malodorous. An unwarranted largesse jeopardising affections.

Incarnations of others! Avatars of aunties or the redistribution of a grandfatherly feature familiarly renowned. Generations jostle for rehabilitation: utter newness not so. It is true too what they say about the ubiquity of politicians: every baby figures, alas, in its features at least one. Old age is also oxymoronically there — in the crumpling of a cry, the aspect of perturbation frowningly announced, the contraction to a body full of bodily obligations.

Perfection is partly in the size of its bundle, exactly rightweight for cuddle, and composed armful-size. So eminently embraceable, so compassed and encompassed, all directions being one. In the snuffle for milk, an arrangement of crescents meet in concise global alignment, well-acquainted and reciprocal. A breath warm, skin confirmed, immediate proximity. There is nothing misplaced in such an arrangement. It has a lover-fit neatness.

Oh, adoration. Summon myrrh-bringing Magi. After anger and tears, stenches, spills, demon vomits and night alarums, the pause-causing frailty of its life-allotted existence. The body curled upon a future. The face waiting for words, for all the impinging everythings still world-held and brain expected. Listening already. Some cortex corrugation prefixed on transmission. Some compulsory complication. Yet there is nothing so simple: heartbeat, heartbeat, heartbeat, heartbeat. The responding, unwombed, star-shaped hand.

At the end of the eighth week the baby was summarily removed to be placed for adoption, and Rose was consigned to the local asylum. It was devastatingly sudden. One day she was there, chattering away over the head of her daughter; the next both were gone, the couple was wrecked and ever-after sundered.

At our first hospital visit I almost did not recognise my elder sister Rose. Bereftness had been for her a kind of death; she was so reduced in body that I wondered if the nurses were systematically starving her. Her skin had a sere, brittle and yellow appearance that I afterwards learned was the result of electricity, her eyes were very fluid, as if verging on tears, her mind irreproachable. Rose's fulsome mouth was quiet and at rest; she had ceased to speak, entered a bleak realm of inversion and vacancy, one in which, not only the mouth, but the whole of her body, had taken on an immobile and vaguely totemic aspect.

I saw my mother smile broadly at her daughter's silence, nod to a nurse who nearby fussed with a teacup.

It was at this stage, I think, that the nightmares began. Typically they concerned my mother's room. I would enter its vegetable, jungle-like shadows, and find her sitting at the dressing-table fingering jewels. Suddenly I would believe myself atrociously electrocuted; my body would blaze for a single instant, my skin would catch fire, wither and become yellow, and at that very moment, the moment in which my own light dispelled the gloom, dead people would appear. The illumined quality of the three planed mirror somehow prismatically conveyed absence to presence, spirit to substance. The most terrible thing was that my sister Rose was numbered among the dead. She, like the others, was extremely thin, and bore an irradiated glow that signified the posthumous. Yet she was not horrific and I would be overcome by a longing to touch and embrace her. At this point the nightmares always concluded the same way. Our mother would intervene to prevent the embrace and Rose would disappear in a spontaneous combustion more complete than my own, a puff! theatrical, leaving nothing more than a spiralling twist of mortuary-grey smoke.

For almost two years Rose's condition remained more or less the same. I thought of spells in fairytales, attitudes of suspension which are both long and transitory and require for release the intercession of magic. (I profaned my mother's room and stole the blue-stoned ring: I turned it and rubbed it, addressed it, prayed to it, held it in the moonlight with invented chants, but all to no avail. I began to fear that any power it possessed was merely material and aesthetic.)

Then, inexplicably, Rose slowly began to register our Sunday visits. I first noticed the change on a dull morning in winter. As I bent to place the usual perfunctory kiss, my loose hair brushed her cheeks and her eyes lifted to mine. Some recognition or moment of verification occurred. Rose's nut-brown eyes forgot their long habit of interior orientation, and focused outwards for a second, linked with my own. A blink certified the barely perceptible shift in consciousness and then tears, many tears, gushed and spilled.

Gradually these signs became more definite and sure, until we looked at each other frankly and wept together heartily. Our mother was ashamed of us. She turned away until the mutual crying had subsided and then, when it was all over and we were publicly recomposed, she would fidget with the teacups, twiddle the teaspoons, and chatter mechanically about nobodies and nothings.

Rose recovered enough to come home for weekends, and it was this newly sanguine sister — still, my mother insisted, dangerously lunatic — who beckoned from the back shed with a tightly curled finger.

See the suns, she whispered.

Come and see the suns!

I paused for a moment, a little afraid. But then I stepped towards her into the shed's deep blue shadow, followed her thin back through the narrow framed doorway and saw the suns. The roof of the shed was of second-hand iron so that it bore in zig-zag rows dozens of nail perforations. The sun outside was at some particular angle that made its light divide beautifully and enter each hole; thus the floor of the shed was spotted all over with tiny yellow suns, accidentally counterfeited. Rose moved around the shed in a kind of trance — as though, entering this place, she had arrived at some personal, private interior — watching the little suns slide along her bare arms and slip in splendid speckles down the fabric of her dress.

Phenomenon mythological! Superabundance of the singular! Stunningly spot-lit at the speed of light. See heavens figure on the palm of my hand. See waves and particles gather in neat circles, the congregation of luminescence, shaft-captured and hole-converged. There are orbs too many to be unremarkable. Division on division in an astronomical propagation.

So intrinsically comic. The self polka-dotted, patterned over clownish. Repetitiousness rampant and referring indiscreetly to teeny weeny bikinis, twirling bow ties or film-star sequences of sequins. This is the infant happiness of the much too much. This is circus superfluity, exceeding bulb boldness. Flashlights! Spangles! Entirely photo-sensitive!

Oh the mirroring multitudes, so splendidly without the incarceration of planes, no cold glassy capture, no mother-eye control. Optics rampant. Visibility, clarity, the winking sheen of mica. Concaves and convexes fashioned instantaneously by shifting, specularly, the body authoritative. I am the body spot bountiful with seven years' good luck!

The decorations of golden. Skin lavished and lit with a coin-precise pigmentation. I am princess bejewelled and wonderfully alchemical. Preciousness settles on the surface of my skin, an elemental simulacrum brilliantly false. No metal quite as bright yet no stringent connoisseur at all unconvinced. A dispersion of luxuriousness ceremonially invested: the slow lowering of crowns, trumpets, cymbals, billions and billions of bold-as-brass buttons.

Caress upon caress. The slide of suns is fingertip analogous. The lover's investigative, comprehensive endearments, the foreplaying familiarity, the gift of plenitude. After a hundred tendernesses I am all antique burnish and you an emissary of dazzling shot silk. I am romanticised summer, fleshly, slumbrous, abundant, satiated, the colour of amber or embers, of afternoons oil-perfumed. The complete, breast heavy, glistering, gilt Venus. Confetti both heathen and matrimonial.

Lights in the eyes. Irises globe daubed. In this is the baby-stare with its consistent mother, its unerroneous, unexpelled spherical reflections. I am the sure satellite of your eyeball surface, the celestial body fluidly shining, the image contained absolutely and with peremptory perfection. Conception. Confirmation. Condensation in rays. Perpetuation in twos and more than twos. Ah, babies!

I stood there at the doorway listening to my sister rave in a mode I can now only describe as ecstatic. She had not spoken in this way since the time of her pregnancy and motherhood. Her voice had a fast and vaguely breathless quality, as though she were subject to slightly different physical laws or a different atmosphere. She pirouetted in a kind of dance that was also strange: both gypsy and aristocratic, abandoned and repressively measured. I was less taken by the suns — a simple natural occurrence — than by the whole sound-and-light show Rose extravagantly presented. It was not histrionic, but seemed authentic and unpractised, a spontaneous, uncontrived, sudden response. I thought of our mother, closeted in her ugly, nightmarish room with the teak box of jewels and the blue-stoned ring. I thought of the absent baby, my niece, rudely confiscated. I remembered the outlandish size of Rose's body, her peaky appearance, her relentless talk. I put my hands to my own face — I cannot say why — and remembered most sharply the three planed mirror, the mirror that, finding in its angles extra vectors of light, installed additional impersonations of one who, in any case, was hardly believable in the original version.

On The Piteous Death of Mary Wollstonecraft

for Marion Campbell

Oh wond'rous words, how sweet they are
According to the meaning which they bring!
Wordsworth, The Prelude (1805)

I

She arises momentarily from the deepsea of unconsciousness, trawls up her drowned mind through fluid dimensions, through shafts of shadow and light, hanging, suspended, like so many false pendulums, emerges, flailing out of the divisible and brimming darkness, and sensing that, after all, she is somehow still alive, involuntarily praises what she no longer believes in: 'Thank God!'

II

She is about to die, this Mary Wollstonecraft. Born in the year of 1759, she will die at thirty-eight of post-partum complications. She is the controversial and august author of *A Vindication of the Rights of Women*. Both famous and feminist in her own uncongenial time. Large-minded. Brave. Of gravity and of substance.

And now her substantiality has found its irrefragably material expression. She is wrecked in some involuted and private part. She is bloody and broken. Succumbing to the banal republic of the body she has become, in her extremity — and her enemies will note it — Woman Incarnate.

III

Memories abound. This is a state of unexpectedly vivid recursion.

It is 1793, Neuilly, France. In the beautiful forest not far from her cottage she lays down in the low grass with her lover, Gilbert Imlay. Her voluminous dress is lifted to her chest, her lacy petticoats flung back in white frothy folds from exposed long drawers and woollen stockings; and now, in the absence of both England and whalebone constraints, she feels entirely fulsome and deliciously wanton. Her garments surround her like exploded petals. She thinks herself Romantic: the lush concavities of the Crimson Rose.

Birch trees filter the shifting sunlight. There is a profound scent of musk and the skitterings of tiny, invisible animals. Leaves, rocking slightly, descend in a series of slow, gust-impelled and noiseless floatations. The breeze is gentle and the ambience illicit.

Mary Wollstonecraft, famous Woman, feels Gilbert Imlay's hand explore with male confidence the various entrances and recesses of her hypocritically modest and well-tied undergarments. Starched cotton and ribbon bows gratefully give way. His touch is soft and his fingers intrepid.

Mary sees Gilbert's face rock rhythmically above her (eyes closed, brow furrowed, a look resembling consternation), and hears him, in sexual distraction, murmur very quietly (using his comic American accent, his low bass tones), she hears him murmur, most distinctly the words 'My God!' His tone is one of pathetic pleasure and Mary supposes, knowing his atheism, that she has been casually deified in the act of sexual congress, that she is not Woman, nor Rose, but Numinous Entity. She smiles to herself. Then she trails her left hand down the body of her lover until, with an audacity purely human, she cups his swaying testicles in the palm of her hand.

IV

The baby. There is a baby from this most recent, still painful wrenching. In moments of lucidity they bring it near, cradling the cocoon-shaped parcel close to her monogrammed pillow.

'Your daughter', they say. 'Your most delicate daughter.'

Mary Wollstonecraft gazes over at the 'William' she had expected, and sees a bluish coloured female with her own immature face. It is impossibly sedate and well composed. When it opens its eyes, on rare occasions, it has a glazed and inward look, focusless, self-concerned and almost solipsistic. Regarding the eyes of her baby, Mary feels superfluous. In its swivelling mirrors she is watery and inhuman.

'Mary', says the midwife, kind Mrs Blenkinsop. 'He has called her Mary.'

From under the mummifying weight and bondage of the bedclothes, tearful Mary Wollstonecraft, now newly eponymous, regards her baby once more.

'A daughter', she whispers. 'Once more a daughter.'

Mrs Blenkinsop notices the ambivalence in her mistress's voice. Mrs Blenkinsop fails to notice, however, that here are evident the symptoms of another subsidence, that Mary Wollstonecraft is busy sliding back into her own body, a body in which, at this very moment, some torment of the womb, some organic agitation, tricks her into thinking that she has not yet delivered, that the sexless baby — its incipient life ready, its blue face furious — still butts rudely against her innards, and that the neat cocoon held nearby is but a fraudulent figment.

V

There is a bewhiskered gentleman who comes and goes and it is

William Godwin, Jacobin husband of five short months of our suffering Mary. She looks directly at his face and summons her own voice to announce in measured sentences that she is doing splendidly, thank you, and that the worst is surely over. He leans above her and descends slowly for a well placed kiss. Mary knows her kissed forehead to be a site of conflagration and spotted with sweat. She imagines herself repulsive.

At first William's face did not appeal. She preferred the other William, the poet and illustrator Blake, or better still his artist companion Henry Fuseli (who was unwisely married). Mary moved among companies of talkative men, disturbed and aroused by passions that were — and how well she knew it — both carnal and intellectual.

This was the scene: Gilbert Imlay was away doing business in Scandinavia and Mary, masquerading for the sake of social acceptance as righteous Mrs Imlay, was in London with their daughter, the French-conceived Fanny. Mary attended dinner parties with the independence of a man. She sat at a table around which mostly eminent couples were disposed, and felt at once wonderfully singular and sadly deserted. William Godwin and Tom Paine were debating Voltaire over minute glasses of sherry. The shibboleth 'Rousseau' echoed throughout the room. Heresies abounded. Heterodoxies and liberalisms everywhere emerged. Humanist dissent rose high into air coloured amber and rendered seductive by lit candelabra. The women at the table were mostly quiet (picking away at morsels of sweet eats, their eyes downcast, apparently observing their own marmoreal bosoms), but Mary Wollstonecraft, alias Imlay, felt compelled to loudly pronounce on the Perfectibility of Man and the Exemplary Necessity of Justice and Reason. Her own voice interceded and made itself known. Male faces turned. Kind William Blake, conspicuously wearing the *bonnet rouge* of the French revolutionists, smiled broadly and lifted his glass at the other end of the table. The women were disquieted. William Godwin raised an eyebrow and begged Mrs Mary Imlay to continue, if she would, her remarkable disquisition within which, with rare conviction, she extended the fine principles of Reason and Equality even to the remote and insular sphere of Womankind...

His face moves away. She can see that he is shocked by some deterioration in her condition. Her sweat appears glistening on the surface of his lips.

'Mrs Godwin, my love', he murmurs miserably. And then he presses her hand, turns and leaves.

VI

They have placed the baby upon her but no milk is forthcoming. Blue that it is, tiny and palpitating, it seems unable to suckle. Mrs Blenkinsop dutifully pummels at her mistress's nipples, fiddles assiduously with the baby's minute mouth, and rearranges their collusion.

Mary closes her eyes and knows, as mothers are reputed instinctually to know such things, that the baby will die. She feels the small weight redistributed upon her chest. The hands of Mrs Blenkinsop. A darkness gathering in her belly most plausibly attributable to premonitions of grief.

Had she been better clairvoyant Mary Wollstonecraft would have known that her daughter Mary would live for fifty-three years and achieve a fame ratified in the twentieth century by that most pompous and preposterous of all institutions, Hollywood. 'The Rights of Women' will historically prove a difficult concept; her daughter's 'Frankenstein', however, is a convenient cultural nightmare, delectably beastly and radiantly terrifying. Adults will flinch and clutch one another in the face of Mary Shelley's confected monstrosity. Children in dark rows will tremble and become intoxicated with fear. Organ music, tenebrous bedrooms, dark-and-stormy-nights, will unaccountably perpetuate.

But now, at this moment, mother Mary can imagine no parturition more terrible, no fiction more cruel, than that which she has recently, factually experienced. She feels she has been gouged.

Blood is somewhere staining the white linen bedclothes. And Mrs Blenkinsop continues, indefatigable and persnickety, to juggle and arrange the uncompliant infant.

VII

In this fluid and rather precarious state she remembers her second attempt at suicide.

Imlay had cast her off, and installed, in hasty secrecy, a mistress in her place. He was indifferent to Fanny, and found Mary Wollstonecraft's Passion alarmingly Presumptuous and Unbecoming of a Woman.

It rained incessantly. She walked into a wet dark so densely streaming that her very substance seemed to yield to the pleasures of dilution. Unsustained by Love she gazed into the accelerating waters of the Thames, the channels and rivulets and ripples of which were gleaming dully under the spectral attention of the floating moon. Battersea bridge was far too crowded, so Mary, Rationally intent, hired a boat to take her further up the Thames to Putney. The boat-master expressed class-conscious surprise: that so decent a woman should be afield and alone on a night such as this! Mary lowered her gaze; she hoped that this deferential, compassionate fellow, with reddish coloured whiskers and scabby hands, would not be the one who, in the morning, with long spiked sticks, would finally skewer and recover her drifting body.

At the second bridge she walked once again in the rain. It was important, she knew, to execute this carefully; waterlogged clothes would expedite quick submersion. She climbed the railing of the bridge and flung herself into the water. Currents embraced her. The cold was extraordinary. But Mary realised, to her dismay, that her large dress had ballooned up around her body, that she was buoyed and bobbed by the semi-globe of her abundant and Womanish clothes. She beat down her bloated dress with frantic impatience and gradually, mercifully, the water began to take her. She felt her mouth inundate. She gulped at the river. She breathed in whole draughts of black liquid to her lungs. And then, complete darkness.

Some instant hero or other foiled this death. Some ordinary Englishman dived into the Thames and dragged the drowning woman — whose clothes, he later remarked, made her exceedingly heavy, not at all the flimsy Ophelia one might be tempted to imagine — and wrenched her dripping body definitively lifewards.

VIII

Godwin is there, hovering beside the candle, head intimately inclined to kind Mrs Blenkinsop. Mary watches them converse in soft hushed tones; they appear conspiratorial, as though they discuss, perhaps, the death of the baby, and are conferring on how best to inform the mother. Godwin also has his look of scholarly perplexity; the famous author of *Political Justice* is perhaps considering in what manner of humane and just terms he might announce to his wife the baby's demise.

But no, she is mistaken. The baby is merely asleep in the cradle beside her, calm and somehow securely life-tenanted. Mary closes her eyes and cannot at all understand the profundity of her sense of closening doom.

Later—but it may have been seconds—the two are still there talking. Mary watches Godwin's mouth and remembers his speeches and writings on the many and various iniquities of marriage. She remembers this statement:

...marriage, as now understood, is a monopoly, and the worst of monopolies. So long as two human beings are forbidden, by positive institution, to follow the dictates of their own mind, prejudice will be alive and vigorous. So long as I seek, by despotic and artificial means, to maintain my possession of a woman, I am guilty of the most odious selfishness.

The despot is fiddling with a gobbet of candlewax. Mary knows she is in Love. She is anti-Rational. She dwells on the lips of the man whom, only recently, her own body enormous with the burgeoning baby, she kissed and kissed to the very brink of obscenity.

IX

Once or twice they brought Fanny into the room to see her. She is a pretty child of precocious intelligence and with a will to survive proven impressively by her early defeat of smallpox. Mary speculates a famous future for her daughter, whom she does not consider in any way illegitimate. She stares at her child and sees Imlay vestigial in its three year old features.

The birth of Fanny had been simple and uncomplicated. After a single day's confinement Mary was up and about, carrying the new baby on walks in the sunshine. She felt, momentarily, completely happy. In a joyous letter she wrote: *'my little girl begins to suck so manfully that her father reckons saucily on her writing the second part of The Rights of Women!'* And she chuckled as her quill sped its words across the page.

The child Fanny now enquires of the whereabouts of William Godwin, whom she oddly and endearingly calls by the name of 'Man'. She seems perplexed by her mother's inexplicable misery, and is, in this perplexity, preoccupied and somewhat fidgety. She runs her small fingers around the monogrammed letters stitched in crème silk upon the white linen sheets: 'M' rightway up and upsidedown.

(Fanny is beginning to assume the quality of 'cadaverous quiet' which Coleridge will later note in the 'Godwin' daughters.)

Finding Man absent, she can think of nothing to say to her ailing mother. She continues tracing the peaks and valleys of the embroidered letters. There is sepulchral silence.

On the ninth of October, 1816, Miss Fanny Godwin, aged twenty-two years, having discovered at last the fact of her Illegitimacy, committed suicide by the ingestion of too much opium. Her name was somehow torn from her suicide note, so that her identity was not recorded in the local papers. William Godwin forbade the claiming of the body. No one, it is recorded, attended the anonymous funeral. And younger sister Mary forgot, apparently, to register the melancholy event in her private journal.

X

Mrs Blenkinsop is leaning above her with a cloth soaked in warm rose water and the attitude of a pietà. Her eyes are remarkably close and concerned. She frowns as she dabs and dabs and dabs, as though committed to the removal of an unseemly public stain spilt upon the brow.

Mary remembers, now, her own long-deceased mother. She remembers Elizabeth Dixon of Ballyshannon, and how, on one of those mortifying childhood nights, she leant above her thus, dabbing and dabbing. Her father had flung, not his fists this time, but a pewter mug. It flew through the air like a bizarre metal weapon — she seemed to see it as though its motion were preternaturally slow, as though the very angle of its descent and rate of its velocity were retarded by Nature for her own terrified inspection — and extended efficiently the arm of brutality. Brown ale sprayed down on them. And then it struck. Mary saw her own mother suddenly blench and topple backwards, heard a clang of collision, witnessed maternal collapse. Edward Wollstonecraft, in response, spat out imprecations and slammed the door behind him. The china objects in the dresser rattled at his exit. Cups tilted and swung. The cat leapt sideways. The whole world, it seemed, was sent constitutionally atrembling in his wake.

At first Mary thought that her mother was dead. 'Dead', she whispered almost salaciously to herself, savouring the word for its stunning finality. But then the woman roused. She uttered arcane syllables which Mary realised were remnants of her indigenous Irish. Sister Elizabeth (always the practical one) appeared with a linen cloth soaked in warm water. And so Mary bent above her mother, dabbing and dabbing at the red blood that welled from the poor woman's wound. There was a pungent stench of ale which, even more than blood, she sought to eradicate. And her mother opened her eyes — they were Mrs Blenkinsop's blue — and whispered, in Irish-inflected tones, 'Ah Mary, me love thank God, thank God'.

The rose water is almost overwhelming in its scent. Striving in her abasement for clear Rationality, Mary decides she must be entering a state of delirium since she could swear that it is blood that is issuing in copious floods from her flaming brow.

XI

For no apparent reason she requests a mirror. 'A mirror, if you please, Mrs Blenkinsop. A mirror.'

So proud, she was. Everyone was speaking of the Rights of Women. Mary posed for another portrait by the artist Sir John Opie, and felt herself becoming more and more substantial by the minute. She had donned her favourite striped gown, placed a simple scarf at her head, and refusing all manner of ornament and frippery, had contrived to appear the very figure of Contemplative Reason. Sir John painted her seated at her own writing bureau; she held open her own book, and turned to the artist as though thoroughly and warmly commending its contents. A quill and an inkbottle, her only accessories, appeared with contrived austerity in the middle distance background.

Mary watched Sir John Opie judiciously dabble his brush, lean back, pause, and lean forward restrainedly to add another brushstroke to her famous countenance. She hoped that the portrait would show her sagacious and earnest. He leant back and forward, forward and back, and Mary's eyes strayed to the page upon which was written, as it happened, a paragraph considered by her critics one of the most unforgivably blasphemous:

Probably the prevailing opinion that woman was created for men, may have taken its rise from Moses' poetical story; yet as very few, it is presumed, who have bestowed any serious thought on the subject ever supposed that Eve was, literally speaking, one of Adam's ribs, the deduction must be allowed to fall to the ground, or only be so far admitted as it proves that man, from the remotest antiquity, found it convenient to exert his strength to subjugate his companion, and his invention to show that she ought to have her neck bent under the yoke, because the whole of creation was only created for his convenience and pleasure.

Mary smiled at her boldness. The 'convenience' of 'subjugation': such a felicitous turn of phrase.

Mrs Blenkinsop has returned. 'Mr Godwin', she announces (in a manner unbecomingly stiff and formal), 'has refused Mrs Godwin all access to mirrors'. Then she bobs a half curtsey, apparently apologetic, turns and retreats.

XII

She knows about death and senses its proximity.

This was a woman, this Mary Wollstonecraft, who from her window in Paris in 1793 had seen King Louis XVI bound tight in a hackney coach on his way to the guillotine. She had walked in the dark streets and found pools of shining blood sprung directly from the necks of counter-revolutionists and Girondins. Tumbrels rumbled in her mind and the triangular blade daily and actually fell. The Terror was abroad, barbarous and behemothic.

In her dank little room Mary recorded for posterity that for the first time in her life she could not extinguish the candle on her nightly retirement. Darkness was already the pervading Genius. She lifted her pen and wondered how Reason had so rapidly evolved to Unreason. Tom Paine was held in a Paris prison — having argued in a tribunal against the King's death — and would miss the guillotine by the merest good fortune. Soon Charlotte Corday would eliminate Marat, and for this act pay with an execution of rare and unprecedented publicity. Mary's dear friend Madam Roland would also succumb. So each night under the candle which she did not dare snuff out, she crossed through those names of her revolutionary comrades who, in a History now adventitious, unamenable and perverse, had been dealt ruination.

Gilbert Imlay appeared. He was miraculously sexual and individual. He spoke with an incontrovertible American accent. Smiled full-teethed in the face of History. Commanded. Seduced. Took control. He suggested removal from the various dangers and despondencies of Paris to a cottage in the forest near the town of Neuilly. Mary gathered up the remnants of her sad life and fled.

Yet even in the circle of her lover's arms, even in the range of his regular breath, in the warm and encompassing regime of his skin, she let the candle burn on, refused its snuffing, let it burn and burn until it deformed, guttered, and sank ever so silently, into its own collapsed wax.

William Godwin and Mrs Blenkinsop are hovering beside the candle, speaking in hushed tones. Perhaps, Mary thinks, the baby has died. Perhaps they are conferring on how easily and how best to convey this sad intelligence to the ailing mother.

XIII

There was never sublimity, but there were books.

In her small home in the town of Beverley in Yorkshire, where she spent the tempestuous years of adolescence, Mary became divided. In the house all was rage. Bodies were vulnerable, minds infirm. Her father externalised his own intemperate misery, tearing madly at curtains, flinging solid objects, upsetting the table. In the corner — for she was always, it seemed, lodged meekly in the corner — mother Elizabeth curled tightly around the body of her sixth baby, who cried and cried and cried evermore. Siblings screamed noisily at the brawls before them. And Mary called upon Heaven, with an immodest conviction of her own Propriety and Virtue, to smite her father dead instantly with a bright stroke of jagged lightning aimed directly at the heart.

Outside was quite Other, and another, more poised Mary came into being. Disencumbered of brothers and sisters and homely iniquities, she would escape to the realm of Nature, and converse privately and specifically with the real father, God. From the top of the hill she could see the mediaeval church of Beverley and its perfect spire. All was right — at some level — with the state of the world. On the outside, too, Mary read quietly and industriously the bundles of books she had borrowed. She cohabited with personages plucked from fiction. She discoursed with philosophers, debated with translated Greeks, dallianced with foreigners, journeyers, God-fearers and reprobates. Sweet, sweet Reason. Outside, under the trees, overlooking the church, far, far from the wailing of several babies, Mary read and contemplated and decided peremptorily — and not, that is, without singular Good Reason — on the far superior claims of the intellect.

XIV

Ah, Godwin. He had enclosed her in his arms. He had gently kissed with his tongue the soft lobe of her ear. He had slid his lips towards hers, rapturously careful, and completed with the gravity of an extenuated kiss. Mary felt herself transform. Her own body was blossoming, becoming sapfilled, convoluted, roseate and petal-like. She opened her eyes and saw that he lay close beside her in a kind of relaxed and glorious repose. Beyond the boundaries of their bed (framed at two ends by iron-work ivy) was a marble wash-stand and jug, a bookshelf crammed with books, drawn curtains of brocade and an oak mantelpiece upon which stood two silver candlesticks and a European clock which swung with sobriety its true and regular pendulum. There was a fireplace just lit, a worn Turkish rug, and a black cat named Jean Jacques curled comfortably spherical. Mary saw it all, this cosy inventory of familiar domestica, with utter lucidity. Not only her own body but the world, too, was suddenly more authoritatively placed in existence, more accomplished, regenerate.

'Mary', he whispered, 'Mary, Mary'.

Then he covered her again, played suavely and attentively at the bloom of her body, coaxed incense, resonance, a totality of swoons.

Later, as they lay apart, he began to joke. Replaying the derisive slander of the English press William Godwin teased her: 'Imperious Amazon', he said half smiling. 'Hyena in Petticoats'; 'Godless Whore'; 'Philosophising Serpent'; 'Shameless Wanton'.

The last he pronounced with such an exaggerated and ingratiating mock distaste that Mary broke into laughter. She leapt in an excess of good humour and pleasure upon her lover's naked body. And the two rolled together, tumbled right off the bed and onto the worn Turkish rug, and turned and turned, subversively hilarious.

XV

Mary can faintly hear the voice of kind Mrs Blenkinsop. 'Dear God', she is saying, 'dear God, dear God', in a tone that sounds very like distress and lamentation.

Mary opens her eyes. Mrs Blenkinsop is standing at the back of the room, and looming above her is Dr Fordyce, who has apparently replaced the midwife's ministrations.

Dr Fordyce is busy arranging, with veterinary firmness, a small brown puppy upon each breast.

'These will draw out the milk', he explains abruptly, noting the patient's return to inquisitive consciousness.

Mary is abased. Mary is quaking and in a state of revulsion. The animals writhe at her chest, imposing anguish. She looks at their paws, their honey eyes, and their tiny tongues, and wonders what has become of her own infant, Mary. She feels animal mouths rudely and frantically suckle. She cannot believe her own body has been thus abused and exposed.

When she is next in consciousness Dr Carlyle is there, and later still the surgeon, Mr Clarke, is in attendance. This is an ominous gathering. They bend above her with looks of studious annoyance. Whisper. Confer.

And she thinks only of the puppies, their warmth, their misplacement, their disgusting hunger.

XVI

Let us not pretend that there is some moment of relief or

restitution. The death is miserable. Godwin tips glass after glass of sweet sherry down her throat, so that it may be said she is becoming absolutely drunken. She sees the room start to reel. Several of her women friends stand in a circle around the bed — Maria, Eliza, Everina, Amelia — and they bear on their faces the prefiguring of her doom. Something in their expressions discloses the irrevocable.

Mary Wollstonecraft raises her eyes to William Godwin, and sees the veins, like graveyard worms, outstanding on his temples. He smiles at her bravely. Mrs Blenkinsop enters the room with an extra lit taper so that more light is cast, and human shadows diminish and waver against the walls.

'Mary', she says, calling out her own name. 'Where then is Mary?'

Mrs Blenkinsop reaches deep into the nearby cradle and retrieves the small infant; the other women all turn, uniform as a chorus, as she brings it over to the bedside.

'Ah, Mary.'

The baby is sleeping. Its eyelids quiver at some inscrutable dream. Mary now actually realises that it has assumed autonomy. It awaits its own history, is poised, alive. It nestles, wholly oblivious, on the edge of the pillow upon which are embroidered its mother's initials.

Mary's two swollen breasts ache terribly from bites and scratches inflicted by the puppies. Her insides are raw, wounded, Womanly. She heaves a sigh and feels the waters begin to close around her. Black ripples appear in the field of her vision. Faces are beginning to seem fluid and indefinite. The room dims and liquefies. Then, complete dark.

XVII

Foolishly confounding Virtue and Truth, William Godwin wrote a memoir of his deceased wife's life. In it he hoped to memorialise the Excellent Woman. He spoke of Imlay, of Fuseli, of suicide attempts, illegitimate birth, sexual passion and intellectual voluptuousness. 'Mary Wollstonecraft' became synonymous with

Villainous Depravity. The Woman was Gross, Unprincipled, Debauched and Scarlet. One Reverend gentleman passed the opinion publicly that death-by-childbirth was God's clear judgement on her Transgression of Womanly Decency. And this was, in some ways, the least of the vilification.

William Godwin retired for several years, sorrowful and confused, to the umbrageous and austere safety of his book-lined study. But from behind his door he fancied that he heard, occasionally, footfalls soft as feathers and curiously ghostly from the two strangely silent, strangely grave, and irreparably motherless daughters of dead Mary Wollstonecraft.

Knowledge

On the remote and tiny island off northern Australia where my mother and father worked as missionaries there was one area of beach I was prohibited to visit. It was, my father explained, some kind of cleansing beach, a place where the Aboriginal people, in times of intolerable distress or guilt, walked into the sea, cast off their clothes, and then, after whatever due ceremony or act of communion, re-emerged naked to the world and mysteriously renewed. I would know this special beach, my father warned, by the odd litter of clothing thrown back by the sea, and if, by chance, I ever came upon this beach, this unusual beach of littered clothes, then I must turn the other way, and walk back to the place from which I had come.

Even then I understood that it was nakedness not sacredness that caused my father's warning. He had no particular respect for Aboriginal culture; indeed he was doing his utmost to dissuade the people from their tribal ways. It was with contempt and with a peculiar contraction of the lips — which seemed to signify an almost physical sensation of disgust — that he spoke of their dances and fights, their sucking at turtles' eggs and scooping at the bellies of fish, their laborious body painting, their elaborate funerals, their night-time descriptions of their own cosmogony. The things that fascinated me he regarded as primitive and in need of conversion. He would shake his grey head and with a melancholy tone of false solicitude lament that the Aboriginal people were insufficiently intelligent to see the wisdom of his ways. To me this opinion was inexplicable: it was only later that I realised that contempt, like hatred, actually explains everything.

This story, I suppose, is of a pair of gloves. They arrived one day at our island community along with dozens of miscellaneous items of cast-off clothes. From time to time white people in the South would send, without warning, large canvas bags which were stamped in red ink with the mysterious legend AIM. The arrival of these bags was always a pleasure and even though I was not permitted to participate in the sharing I enjoyed watching the people unpack and distribute each item of clothing according to scrupulous and cunning codes of fairness and need.

We gathered beneath the mango tree that grew behind the church, sat ourselves down in a rough circle upon the dirt, and a nominated woman — usually Mary Magdalene — would, with great solemnity and purpose, cut open each bag and reveal its gifts. Unseasonable sweaters (left behind after football matches), copious floral frocks (discarded, presumably, after slimming routines), tee shirts (washed unwisely to a state of unflattering shapelessness), trousers (from dead men), shoes (out of fashion), skirts, blouses, even suspenders: all sprung from the AIM bag, carrying with them their ghostly implications of invisible lives lived in faraway places. Mary Magdalene would dangle each item for a brief inspection, and then after laughter, exclamations, suggestions and contestation, nominate decisively the new recipient. Being a person of suave and subtle command she was rarely contradicted.

On the day of the gloves I recall that there were two other unusual items on display. The first, which was greeted by a shriek of embarrassed giggles, was an extraordinary gown which I took to be a wealthy woman's nightie or petticoat. It was pearl-coloured, diaphanous and intricately gold-threaded, and Mary Magdalene flung it over our heads to a young woman named Rebekah, who was about to be married. Rebekah, I remember, held the lovely petticoat across her hips, shyly exhilarated; and then catching by accident the gaze of her lover, buried her face in its folds, mock-virginal and pleased.

The other item of clothing, one even more fabulous and strangely dislocated, was an ancient fox fur, the type that women in magazines might wear draped at their necks. This object caused a general stir of consternation, and Mary Magdalene seemed wholly unsure of its use. She held the fur at arm's length and sent a small child to summon old-man Francis Xavier for his wisdom and advice. He arrived, examined the fur, and declaring in his own language that it was nobody's totem, flung it ostentatiously to the waiting dogs. Commotion erupted as the animals tore at the fur and above us black flying foxes shuddered in the mango leaves and shifted their shapes nervously in response to the din.

All of the clothes had apparently been displayed and distributed, the flying foxes had resettled, the dogs, disconsolate, lay resting in the dust among little fragments of now unidentifiable fox, when Mary Magdalene upended the last of the AIM bags to reveal a pair of gloves. They plopped gently at her feet, like two pathetic hands in weary supplication; they were white and embroidered and struck me as objects of the most astonishing delicacy. I had never in fact seen a pair of real gloves before, and they were so ingeniously hand-like, so redolent of another order where even fingers are clothed, where one touches fastidiously and points and caresses beneath a smooth enveloping surface, elegantly drawn on, digit by extended digit — drawn on, no doubt, to the accompaniment of whining violins and curling wreaths of blue-grey smoke — so redolent were these gloves that I longed to possess them. They were distinctively otherworldly, foreign, adorable. Wall-papered interiors opened in my mind. There were velvety surfaces, embossed upholstery and high-toned tinklings from prismatic glass. And from somewhere unseen in this private province a copper light entered, bringing peach tones to the furniture and pretty moon-shaped shines to the surfaces of paperweights and burnished vases...

I knew from experience that such impractical objects as gloves would not be valued by the community, and, as it happened, I was absolutely correct. There were a few faint murmurs of curiosity, but no one seemed to think that they were at all worth claiming.

To my surprise, however, Mary Magdalene took up the gloves and with no consultation stuffed them pre-emptively in the front of her shirt and declared the clothes distribution over. There was no sense in which this was a crudely appropriative gesture; she simply took the unwanted gloves and efficiently dismissed us.

My heart began to swell in self-conscious anger. There were inner ructions and disturbances which registered — how shall I put it? — the childish beginnings of the sin of covetousness.

I am not sure, even now, why the gloves so entranced me, but I think it may have been connected to a visit to the cinema. Once when I was seven, or perhaps six years old, I flew with my mother in the small mail plane south-west across the sea to the town of Darwin. The actual purpose of our visit was a new set of maternal dentures, but to me it centred entirely on a promised cinematic occasion.

The movie that we saw — illicitly, given my father's beliefs — was in black and white, but utterly impressive. It was like a kind of dreaming, fluid and non-participatory, effortless and ineluctable. And there, dreaming awake, in the warm embrace of darkness, I saw in gigantic projection the most brilliant of scenes and occurrences. An unknown city. Houses of impossible and imposing solidity filled to the brim with objects from storybooks. There were singing and dancing and beautiful Audrey Hepburn. There were men with heads thrown back as they smoked slim cigarettes, women in hats and gloves who peered over their sunglasses, cars without roofs and scarves in the wind, gyrations on dance floors and bristling intimacy, and one long orchestrated kiss, breathtakingly held. I sat wholly agape, stunned by what my mother later called 'civilisation'.

(And she forbade me absolutely to tell my father of the movie. Our own little secret, she whispered in my ear.)

When I saw the gloves from the AIM bag perhaps I recalled certain images from the movie several years before. More puzzlingly, though, I was simply consumed by an unpremeditated desire, by a kind of imprecise longing, stringent as hunger. For days I could think of nothing but the gloves, and moved through the community annoyed and preoccupied. Mary Magdalene, whom I had loved, became the special object of my anger and ill-feeling, yet I did not ask her for the gloves — somehow it never occurred to me — I simply resented her possession.

At night I lay beneath my mosquito net listening to the Aboriginal songs arising through the dark from the campsite beyond our fence. Clapsticks struck and voices rose. I listened to the cycles of tribal chants telling of ancestors and rainmaking, and I thought, not as usual of the conjured images of the songs, of sweeping monsoons bending low the pandanus, of the spearing of dugong or the transformation of sisters into stars or birds; I thought instead of a white woman who, with long gloves, moved in slow motion down a curved flight of stairs and accepted a triangle shaped glass in a gesture of haughty and experienced seduction. This woman of my imagining wore a diaphanous petticoat and a fox fur at her throat, but her distinction, her supremacy, her all-time claim-to-fame, was marked most specifically by her dazzling gloves. I heard the voices through the night, mythological and familiar, and constructed, as though in some kind of strict competition, my immaculately gloved woman to contest and denounce them.

The gloves disappeared for several weeks but then reappeared conspicuously at Rebekah's wedding. Weddings were insisted upon by the mission authorities, but the people of the island treated them with a mixture of vague derision and half-hearted enthusiasm.

Mary Magdalene attended the wedding wearing my pair of white gloves. I remember thinking how ludicrous and misplaced they looked, how they were unsuited to black skin, how rather than clothing or ensheathing her arms they appeared stuck on and superfluous. My envy was huge. I sat in the middle row between my friends Rachel and Hepzibah and became gradually aware—quite unexpectedly—of something anomalous and odd in my situation. It was not anything which I could comprehend or even identify, it was some minor revelation of disjunction or difficulty, a feeling which, in my pique, I was able to hastily attribute to Mary Magdalene's too-flagrant exhibition of my gloves. But as I sat in the pew, suddenly everything appeared particularly concentrated and clear, so that now I remember the wedding scene in each exact, perspicuous detail.

A yellow light fell brightly through the doors of the church — for it was little more than a shed, mostly open at both sides — and lay across the earth floor, not quite reaching where my father stood. There was an altar decorated in Aboriginal designs, with X-rayed fish and patterns of cross hatching, and above it a wooden cross, robustly hewn. My father stood before the altar with the bible in his hands; he was robed and authoritative, and spoke in an unusual and extremely loud voice, as though the church were not of bark but some vaulted and echoing cathedral of marble and stone. I remember thinking for the first time: my father is annoyed; this is a voice of annoyance; this is unholy, improper.

Before my father kneeled Rebekah and Jacob Njabalerra, she in the communal wedding dress which I had seen several times before and which now barely contained her swelling stomach, he in a new-secondhand AIM shirt of cowboy checks. Both Rebekah and Jacob were bent low before my father as though receiving remonstration. My mother, I noticed, was seated in the very front row of the church and she too was bent over. Her head was bowed and submissive and I somewhat precociously thought: this is as she always is, my mother bowed thus, hunched before my father. The nape of her neck appeared exposed and pitiable and my unclear sense of disjunction resolved around its image.

I instantaneously felt what I can only now describe as the profundity of dissent. I hated my father. I hated his voice as it married the couple. I hated the rustle of his robes and the largeness of his hands. His deliberative actions. His presence. His face. I was pleased to be sitting at a critical distance.

It was at this point that Mary Magdalene turned and smiled indulgently and waved a gloved hand at me. Sitting next to her

Joseph, her older husband, also abruptly turned, as though curious to see what had caught his wife's attention. He too gave me a wave, spontaneously complicit with Mary Magdalene's offering. Beside me Rachel and Hepzibah snickered a little, but I was caught in a moment of confused response. Anger and envy competed with shame. I felt ungenerous and mean. I raised my arm to wave back to Mary Magdalene — it seemed so proper an action, so reciprocally incumbent — and felt the burdensome gloved woman poised on the staircase inside my head begin to insubstantially waver and disperse. I smiled at Mary Magdalene and she continued to smile at me. I saw the lustrous and shining dark of her half-turned face and thought — I remember now — how beautiful her skin was, how it caught, with perfect ease, bows of glaze and illumination from even that shadowy and church enclosed air.

I did not entirely relinquish a hankering for the gloves — my cinema woman's residency was much too tenacious — but reconciled with Mary Magdalene and resumed fishing and gathering food with her. We never spoke of the gloves at all, and I believe she may have guessed that these were the particular, shameful cause of my previous bad humour. It was a subject which remained between us like an invisible canoe. We moved slightly apart, were gentle with each other and tentative in our behaviour. It was as though we balanced a weight, each aware of the poise and co-operation of the other.

Within weeks after the wedding, however, this poise was lost: Mary Magdalene was cast into a terrible despair. Her husband Joseph had been beaten with a nulla-nulla in a fight, and at his death she collapsed into a state of voluble grief, one so extreme in its expression that I dared not approach her.

The mourning cries trailed throughout the campsite. Even closed in our house I heard traces of her voice, eerie and miserable and continuously plaintive. I knew too that Mary Magdalene would be cutting her breasts with stones and tearing distractedly at her hair as she had done, several years before, when her only daughter had died. There was of course also a chorus of other women mourners, but her single voice rose above them and attested a more immediate and individual pain. I could not bear the wailing. I thought of the ash-smeared face and the blood upon her breasts, the body doubled over at a diligent self-mutilation.

Yet it was at dinner time, I remember, when in my own copycat misery, my own version of imagining Mary Magdalene's awful condition, that I insulted finally and irreparably the paternal order of things. My father sat above his meat, stabbing and sawing, and then announced with undisguised impatience and anger:

'Why doesn't that woman shut up? Why must she go on?'

And since I knew the correct answer from Rebekah Njabalerra I could not remain silent.

'Because she fucked Peter Moorla before he killed Joseph.'

There was a dreadful, static silence. My father swallowed his mouthful. My mother hung her head, wretched at my mistake and blushing excessively. And then father arose, thumped at the table, and shouted in a voice I still continue to hear:

'You know nothing at all! Nothing! Nothing!'

He struck the side of my head with such rude intensity that my ear dramatically exploded with blood. Then he strode from the room and was absorbed almost instantly into the gathering darkness.

I did not see Mary Magdalene walk into the sea but I know that she did because I found the gloves at the clothes beach. And although I did not see her I believed I could reconstruct in every single detail exactly what happened.

In the movie in my head she approached the waves very slowly, hesitating at first as though somehow assessing their qualities. Then she would proceed, moving deeper, until the water flowed in gentle eddies and soothing circuits around her body. Her clothes would become liquid and begin to rock against her skin. Then she would submerge entirely, and after a second or two arise, her black skin glistening and bright with rivulets of water, to stretch up her arms and remove her large, loose dress. Then, last of all, she would pull each white glove from each black hand and set them floating beside her, like phantom remnants of another body or some unimaginable life form. She would stay for a few minutes naked in the water, her cut breasts stinging with the salt water, her hair streaming out behind, and then walk back through the waves, slowly and ritualistically. In my vision it was a dark and monsoonal day, so that the sky was grey and the water deep purple. But the remarkable feature of the scene was that despite the lack of light Mary Magdalene's skin was almost blazing with silver. Her nakedness was magnificent.

I cannot exactly recall when I discovered the clothes beach. I had walked much further than usual in the direction I suspected, when I came unprepared and unforewarned upon it. There, in a little bay, feeling at once vaguely treacherous and certainly transgressive, I suddenly saw them. One glove was draped rather tremulously in the mangroves and the second lay, at a small distance, beneath it in the sand. I contemplated the gloves, so vibrantly white, so innocently tide-cast, and realised at once that I knew something with certitude. I knew that the gloves were incorporated into another realm. They were no longer recoverable, no longer desirable, no longer in fact white. The gloves on the clothes beach — formerly so invested with my movie-tone visions — were absolutely transfigured, remade Aboriginal.

Touching Tiananmen

It is a rare kind of fear, and an experience common to many travellers, that one awakens in the night in a state of absolute lostness. Furniture in the room is mere strange monuments, dimensions of windows and walls are false or incalculable, and the surrounding darkness seems simply to confirm displacement. It is a riveting shock: one sits bolt upright, like some monster in a movie, new to the very world.

Anna sat thus, lost in space. Her heart banged in her body and she watched, half-dreaming, the vague room of her small hotel bevel and shift and fail to settle around her.

'China, Beijing', she whispered to herself — as though the words themselves might fix things finally, and in fact they did. The room halted and stilled; Anna adjusted her vision to the darkness, saw her luggage in the corner, recalled the position of her room, the face of the hotel manager (perpetually smiling), the facade of the hotel (fifties-totalitarian), the situation of the building in relation to the city centre, the highway, the bicycles, the many statues of Mao. China, Beijing — no delusion at all but an actual city, inveterate and substantial, and in which she now sought her annual vacation.

Like most cities it had been pre-empted by many versions. When Anna was driven that first day away from the airport she almost expected a skyline of pagodas. She had imagined vistas of lacquered roofs curled imploringly to the sky, tier upon tier of them. Some prospect rather like a willow-pattern plate, but one coloured scarlet and with embossed lettering of gold. Trailing cranes. A pond. The bow of a neat bridge. Mountains unreal and without perspective. And there was, or so it seemed, no origin to this vision; it was simply a confederation of cultural clichés, derived from who-knows-where and mysteriously insistent.

She sat in the rickety airport bus and saw through its glassless window not pagodas at all but a dense green wood of unfamiliar trees from which issued the drumming of millions of hidden crickets. And further on, into the city, rows of tall grey apartments, most of which were unkempt and in various states of dilapidation, and beside them public buildings of truly ostentatious ugliness. These had a state sponsored gigantism, a quality also evident in statues and posters of Mao which, unmet by the recent Soviet-style iconoclasm, persisted in their confident, moon-faced presence. Mao smiled hugely everywhere; he beamed from hoardings and school yards, in stores and on buses. Or he gestured to the future in marble poses. Something severely utilitarian governed Beijing; Anna felt almost deceived; she wondered where the exotic decoration was secreted.

There were of course touristic dimensions to the city; and within the first week of her visit Anna had trudged dutifully in and out of Imperial palaces (noting that opulence for which revolution was finally the only response), climbed arduously and achingly a few kilometres of the Great Wall (recalling Kafka's perverse version within which he alleged it to be the foundations of the Tower of Babel), gawked inside temples (touched by the melancholy of the mere handful of monks who now attended them, by the Mao-looking buddhas, also gigantic), and searched out those few stores whose task it is to supply Westerners with trinkets and superfluities (ah, the brilliancy of cloisonné, the statues of jade, embroidered silk nightware and ornaments of lapis and coral).

But she remained somehow disappointed. Alone and monolingual, she was aware that she dealt merely in pre-visions and exteriorities. She knew no Chinese people, and walked among them like a kind of object, conspicuous but inhuman, inaccessible to them as they were to her, without insides, a doll. And when she had accomplished one by one the tourist locations, she was left curiously unsated and felt almost a physical hunger growing within her.

Anna did not leave Beijing at her travel-agent appointed time. She lingered, without particular cause or purpose, moving first to a smaller and less expensive hotel (that of the fifties-totalitarian facade), delaying her flight to Hong Kong again and again. She became suspended, as it were, in her own unidentified species of longing. Days were spent in the hotel room, lying behind shutters in the false luxuriousness of her new silk lingerie.

Then she began tentatively to venture, down the *hutongs*, or backstreets, in which were to be discovered little buildings, whole little communities, that existed almost in the crevices of the modern city. Below looming apartment blocks were remnants of shanty houses made of sticks; and away from the Chairman's smirking invigilation lives recovered their unbureaucratic disorder. Communal televisions blared loudly at squatting groups. Hawkers pushed handcarts of peaches or spinach. Tailors worked outside at ancient treadle sewing machines and old men and old women meditatively smoked. Children dragged toys or engaged in mock battles. Everywhere were bamboo birdcages placed to entrap crickets, and meat of extraordinary redness hung on hooks at windows.

As Anna lost herself there, irretrievably foreign, she felt the gazes of others resting upon her, like the lightest of touches on the nape of the neck, like a lover's caress. And when the gazes at last accumulated to the point of disturbing her, she would make her way back to the main roads, and there trace a route back again to the hotel.

The city became gradually stranger and stranger. At first, appearing both pagoda-less and high-rise-full, it had seemed comprehendible. But Anna began by degrees to perceive its particularities. The bicyclists of Beijing, seven million or so, moved processionally everywhere: in their inordinate numbers and slow-moving continuity they gave the city a kind of animated and silken effect, recalling a rippling of fabric, a perpetual motion of undulation. And the sound of crickets, which had at first seemed simply a quality of the forest, became ubiquitous. Even at the very centre of the city Anna could hear them. They were an invisible presence, rising, every now and then, to murmurous notice.

Human language also seemed somehow to have altered. Initially Anna had thought she understood the shape of Chinese, its intonations of inquiry, of affection, of polite conversation; but the more keenly she listened the more the language was complicated, the more sounds and circuitous patterns it contained. Her hope of achieving a tiny vocabulary of a few pragmatic phrases faded entirely away. She found herself feeling muted, without language at all. Only in her dreams did she speak Chinese, and then it was of some imperial and antique form, denoting not equitable discourse but that of a foreign devil somehow evilly collusive with old regimes.

As the language multiplied so too did the people, and Anna became overwhelmed by the sheer number of different faces she saw around her. The old woman who sold iceblocks from a tub-on-wheels at the corner, the man who each morning led a Mongol pony dragging a cart filled with watermelons, the youths at the hotel who smoked illicitly in clusters and then jerked to attention, mock deferential, as she passed: all these people now seemed possessed of captivatingly individual features. Anna found herself staring, as though some secret would yield itself if one of these faces opened up to her.

She had never before felt so irreparably lonely.

One Beijing day, a day in which that loneliness hugged her closely like a net, she re-visited, on impulse, Tiananmen Square and the Forbidden City. In the square itself all was festive and bright. Family groups sucked on icecreams and children flew kites that trailed dragon shapes with fantastical tails. Photographers had set up stalls covered over by umbrellas and with old-fashioned looking cameras snapped groups of people in what to Anna appeared exaggerated poses.

She stood behind one photographer and looked with his vision: a family of five — parents, apparently, with their over-indulged product of the One Child Policy, a girl of about seven, be-ribboned and be-frilled, another adult, perhaps the aunt, and an old woman in peasant black, the putative grandmother. Behind them, in the distance, was the threading apparition of Beijing bicyclists flowing westwards and eastwards, and beyond them the crimson gates of the Forbidden City, surmounted by an enormous square portrait of Mao and framed at each side by four huge red flags. Anna lowered herself to the tripod's height — all the better to see photographically — and noticed then that the parents were gesturing to her. They were calling her over to be included in their family snapshot and the photographer turned around to add his own cheerful invitation. Anna felt herself blush. She took a place in the group — between the aunt and the mother — and was instantaneously memorialised, there, anonymously, in Tiananmen Square. Members of the family bobbed, smiled and spoke Chinese; Anna retreated with uncivil haste.

As she roamed the square, singular and Occidental, Anna began to fancy that she was being followed. She looked back from time to time and there, indeed, was a young man upon her tracks, a man whose face had a distracted and agitated look, as though he himself was anxious or under surveillance. Anna wove a little in her path, like some devious spy, only to turn again and find she was correct in her surmise: the man still followed. She halted, summoned her courage, and walked back to confront him. The man shuffled uneasily and looked embarrassed.

'Amerika?', he promptly asked.

'Australia', Anna answered, pleased at least that this man could converse in English. But then, quite unprovoked, he seized both her hands and with a kind of madman's intensity mumbled some sort of enigmatic slogan.

'Yoon faw, yoon faw.'

Anna was alarmed. She broke free and ran; she stumbled over flagstones and headed, heart pounding, in the direction of the Forbidden City. When she slowed to look back the man had disappeared, absorbed into the crowd of milling people, itself unimpressed and indifferent to her flight.

From the lookout on the gate Anna peered over the square. She could see parti-coloured circles of umbrellas, people in holiday groups, and a contingent of Red Army soldiers, identifiable by their khaki uniforms and little caps, gathering casually at the Martyr's Memorial in the centre.

This was where, only one year ago, hundreds of thousands of students had taken up occupation. This was where a styrofoam Statue of Liberty, ten metres high, had been utopianly erected. This was where the military had murderously advanced through the darkness. Where tanks had entered and bayonets been raised. Anna found herself scanning the vista for tell-tale signs, for blood stains or tank tracks, not knowing the square had been re-paved after the purge. Then she began to feel ill. She was aware of repressing memories derived from television: she would simply not allow herself to consciously recollect. Below her all was sunlit and apparently ahistorical. Bicycles moved along the Avenue of Eternal Peace, entrammeled in their own lanes and glidingly unreal. The sound of crickets drifted upwards from emerald coloured trees.

Anna entered the Forbidden City as though seeking refuge. The Imperial buildings were so arranged as to imply security: she passed through gate after gate, through hall after hall, up and down series of steps and across numerous courtyards — architecturally it connoted an almost tyrannical orderliness. Geometrical. Severe. Contrived to express both the physical and metaphysical supremacy of each emperor.

It was also a site where Westerners were known to congregate. Anna roamed the crowds and chose to linger behind a group of German tourists whose leader pronounced on everything in a tone of schoolmasterish annoyance. The tourists were quiet and subservient, and one or two turned to smile at Anna as though she were a long-lost German. From somewhere nearby fragments of English commentary came drifting on the breeze:

> 'The vermilion colour of the walls is achieved by an admixture of pig's blood...'

but Anna was reluctant to accede to the explanations of her native tongue, or to join actually or in spirit the group of Americans so addressed.

Anna drifted away from the Germans and wandered among the more numerous Chinese through the Hall of Preserving Harmony past the Nine-Dragoned Wall, into the Pavilion of Pleasant Sounds, losing herself in pagodas triumphally layered and curved, in room after room of palatial exotica. There were golden bells, extravagant timepieces and ceramic urns of exquisite artfulness. Blackwood furniture, latticed and carved, stood sombrely in corners and upon it were silk draperies embroidery-emblazoned with heavenly beings, phoenixes or brilliant clusters of chrysanthemums. Whole worlds had been carved of varieties of jade, the histories of which were related painstakingly on scrolls. There were astronomical instruments of brass, costumes of opera singers and eunuchs, and jewellery fashioned from every imaginable precious metal and stone. In one hall was a kind of funerary pagoda, perhaps two metres high and of solid gold, in which were retained fingernail clippings and cut hair of the Empress dowager. Oddities, spectacles, artifacts preposterous.

This was a peculiar alienation, to be wandering alone, excommunicated, among so many immoderate objects. Anna had visited this place before, but was now struck for the first time by its quality of obsessive artifice. Everything seemed covered over, embellished, fabricated or beautified. She felt both awestruck and suffocated, both enchanted and repulsed.

Anna made her way rather quickly through the remaining pavilions and halls seeking out the exit that was somewhere ahead, but found herself halted in a small courtyard that she could not remember having seen before. An Englishman was standing before a small stone circle lodged in the earth, and was apparently narrating a story to an assembly of old women:

> 'One day — this was in 1900, almost the end of the Ching Dynasty — the Empress dowager was so annoyed with her daughter-in-law's, the Princess's, reforming zeal and rebelliousness, that she arranged her execution. In the dead of the night four of her eunuchs stole silently into the splendid bedroom, seized the Princess, and

dragged her screaming to the well. Imagine, if you will, the cries in the night, the pleas of the woman as she was stuffed, headfirst, into this tiny hole. As she drowned. In the darkness.'

Anna glanced again at the stone circle, and around it the rather melancholy group of old women, then hastily walked away.

Anna began to visit Tiananmen Square each and every day. She had no particular reason to do so, but was in some way drawn to experience again and again the disconcerting sense of a place which was historically amnesiac, which had obliterated its recent past so utterly and so efficiently. She could not have said why this phenomenon so strangely fixated her: she was simply adrift in another country, caught, after all, in the illusion of a continual, sufficient present. Otiose. Unmotivated.

She walked the large square and mingled, as though indigenous, with the camera-happy crowd at their summer-time leisure. There was always a long line of people — whom Anna assumed to be waiting to see Chairman Mao somewhere embalmed in his crystal casket — but otherwise there was the pleasurable roaming of groups such as occur anywhere in public domains. She watched the kite-fliers and the soldiers, the families and the publicly tentative lovers.

And each day, moreover, she watched the young man. Like her he regularly visited the square. He was always there somewhere, and some days he noticed her presence and some days he did not. Anna never approached the man, nor he she, but began to look out for him, as though to locate his figure in the crowd was the actual purpose of each visit. She would buy an iceblock or a roasted corn cob and trail between groups, leaving after an hour or two; and only once she had sighted the object of her search.

It was on, perhaps, the sixth or seventh day that the young man approached her. With no subterfuge at all he simply walked directly to greet her, as if a meeting had been arranged. He stood there before her and Anna noted that he had a kind of haunted aspect to his face. He was handsome, lean, his skin beautifully ginger, but there was also some quality of despair, of prepossession. Anna imagined for a moment that this man would become her friend, that he would guide, translate, and at last open up the secrets of Beijing.

But in an extraordinary repetition — shocking now precisely because it had a precedent — the man seized both Anna's hands and again chanted out the slogan:

'Yoon faw. Yoon faw.'

She did not break away, sensing this time that the act was not aggressive or threatening, but simply inexplicable. Yet as the man noticed that she had failed to understand his words, he became distressed.

'Yoon faw', he repeated. And he pulled Anna's wrists downwards so that her hands actually made contact with the warm paving stones. Then the man broke into tears, released her, and left.

Anna had a nightmare in which she roamed the Forbidden City on a pitch-black night. She was entirely alone, but around her drifted the most splendid objects: ceramic vases, silk garments, carvings of ivory and jade. As she made her way through the darkness these objects seemed to flow with her, as if held in mystical orbit by her body or her movement. She came at last to a room in which she saw the golden pagoda that she recalled from waking inspection contained fingernails and cut hair. But as Anna moved closer to the pagoda — it seemed to draw or compel her — the dream instantly shifted mode and she saw enacted before her the tale of the princess drowned by eunuchs. There was the dowager Empress looking on, and there was the struggling woman, screaming out her own doom. The four eunuchs, gloriously homicidal in ivory silk, seemed effortlessly to contain and transport the princess: they moved in dream motion, as if mounted on wheels. And though the prisoner writhed, caught in her mobile human frame, the Empress simply stood, regnant and cruel.

Anna watched the scene at first, but then became a participant. However she was not at all sure which character she played. She was simultaneously the evil dowager and the tragic princess; she was either or both; she was hideously divided. And as the woman was thrust down the well (both herself and not herself) there was a cataclysmic sound as the floating objects, their spell broken, came crashing to the ground.

So here is Anna, aroused in the night, and having uttered the words 'China', 'Beijing', relocated in that city. Awakened by lostness she now calmed her fear, becoming sensible and still. She felt suddenly a certain self-contempt and recrimination, that she had stayed so long in Beijing, wasting time and money, so aimless and indulgent. She sat in her bed and thought of her wanderings, of her visits to the square, her mis-spent days.

Then, quite unexpectedly, she realised what it was that the young man had been saying; she solved the riddle of his slogan. The young man — and how could she have missed it, how could she have been so obtuse — had been saying 'June four'; he had been commemorating the date upon which the Tiananmen massacre occurred. Anna had idiotically misunderstood.

Anna lay back on her bed, swathed in silk. She resolved to leave, to fly to Hong Kong. She closed her eyes, longing, passionately longing, for Orientalist clichés, for a city wholly of palaces, pagodas, bowed bridges and trailing cranes. Without history. Without the square. Without the young man, whose image she could not now eradicate.

These Eyes

If thou wilt weep my fortunes, take my eyes.
... Thou must be patient; we came crying hither:
Thou know'st, the first time we smell the air
We wawl and cry ...

King Lear IV, vi.1

The man sitting opposite Paulina is reading *King Lear*. He stepped in at the last stop, found his seat discreetly without at all glancing around, and with, it seemed, that kind of suave self-enclosure possessed by priests and librarians simply opened his book.

He is apparently unaware of the flagrant oddity of this gesture, of its unAustralianness: that a man on a suburban train, rocking its cargo of tired souls from the city in the evening through a bland, undeviating route sketched out like a beaded necklace in small diagrams over the doorways; that a man on such a train — given over, after all, to utility, containment and strict regulation — should so casually read Shakespeare. It is a singular act. It has a certain stupidity or temerity. A certain novelty of dislocation. There are newspaper readers, of course, flicking open the pages or scanning tiny rectangular narratives of murder and mayhem, and there are also, here and there, blockbuster devotees, hunched in positions of engrossed concentration. But this man is enacting in his head a five act Elizabethan drama of the most verbose, intolerable and high-cultural misery. He is silently reeling out dialogue, impersonating a dramatis personae of kings and lords, fools and princesses, the traitorous, the faithful, the vicious and the innocent. He is inwardly transmigrating through character after character, shifting disembodied through a series of avatars and incarnations. He zig-zags between personages, creates unheard blank verse, lonely soliloquies and silent, exclamatory lines of terrible lamentation.

Paulina, let us be frank, is transfixed by this man.

She observes him carefully. His vicinity is such that she can both summarise his whole shape, and yet also detect those fine details usually reserved for a lover's scrutiny. Overall he has a kind of integrity to his bearing, one granted, perhaps, by the autism of reading. He unselfconsciously slouches, but in such a way as to seem to refer to a more comfortable seat, as though his body recalls a familiar reading position that is more habitual and private. He is dressed indistinctly; that is to say Paulina finds it difficult to discern any clues as to profession or social standing. Too poor to be an academic — there is a certain shabbiness to his appearance, and his shirt is white and long-sleeved and therefore possibly clerkish — he is also, apparently, too old to be a student, bearing, as he does, traces of silver-grey in perceptibly thinning hair. He wears unfashionable corduroy trousers and shoes of brown leather. There is no brief case or bag; the only accessory is the book.

The face is beautiful. It is a foreign face, a face, that is, that Paulina thinks immediately is in some way or in some measure migrant. It is long with a large and aquiline nose and bears generous lips, slightly unsealed. There is a pallor which Paulina imagines to be middle European: people from places like Prague or Budapest, she seems to recall, carry the colours of their city upon their faces; they are defined by location, assume the greys and blues of stone buildings and statues, ever after announce their contiguity with certain cityscapes always fixed mysteriously in the spectrum of winter. The man's eyes confirm this: although she can see them only in arcs behind lids and lashes Paulina knows these are the eyes of a man who has looked at the world through the obliterations of snow, who has lived under penumbral European skies and who squints in disbelief at Antipodean summers. These eyes, which are chestnut, move slowly beneath the lids. They slide left to right in limpid and continuous absorption of each long, anfractuous line. There is an inexplicable ease in this act of reading so that Paulina thinks of the phrase 'learned-by-heart' and wonders if, in fact, the man is an actor (she imagines a coffee-coloured dressing room with lines of mirrors studded with light bulbs and containing, in receding perspective, multiplied versions of his face); or if, just as plausibly, he is some sort of wretched autodidact for whom the very name William Shakespeare promises metaphysical solace and incontrovertible gravity (and here she conjures an austere room with a modest shelf of books, a single chair, not unlike Van Gogh's, and a fan-shaped light issuing diffusely through a half-opened door). In any case the man continues to read, secure in his invisible, autonomous life, secretive and oblivious to her speculations.

The train within which this unreciprocated observation takes place is hot and noisy. It is a summer's eve, and the air is hung with commingling odours of sweat and cigarette smoke, both of which are intensified by conditions of rush-hour proximity. A metallic straining and screeching pervades the train which, though impressively automatic and not yet old, shudders with a kind of creaturely death-rattle again and again at each halt upon its journey. The man does not look up from his book as the train buckles and pauses; he is caught in an elsewhere more ineluctably persuasive. He is on the moors with King Lear, or in the castle of Gloucester, or lost, flower-bedecked, in a field somewhere near Dover. Paulina tries to read in his face an exact location, but finds that she cannot; and her incertitude, though reasonable, undermines and destabilises her.

Outside is a world made slippery with speed — tin fences, houses, embankments of yellow grass, elongated shadows cast blankly by billboards, a light, in flashes, of that peculiar fleeting period when afternoon brass disperses to evening mauve — and Paulina is visited all of a sudden by her own obscure melancholy. The man with *King Lear* has occasioned three separate reflections which she disentangles now and sets out before herself as though selfhood were merely a matter of poised accounting and enumeration, as though being a teacher of English literature with a name and a reputation — for solicitous treatment of students, for flighty opinions and inordinate shyness — was not substantially or essentially what she was, but these insurgent moments, coincident always with a kind of idiosyncratic sadness (yet vague, aleatory, in many ways minor), and always requiring, to some degree, acknowledgement and attention, marked most specifically her actual condition.

The initial reflection (and how she smiles to glimpse it, how very private it seems in this train all a-rattle) is of an erotic fantasy. Paulina is in love with a married man to whom, as a consequence of their absolute estrangement, she directs hours of irresponsible and irrepressible longing, many of which moments form themselves, like animated snapshots, in sexual imaginings of elaborate acts of tenderness. She realises now that the most flagrant and lusty of all her fictions is less glorious than a single and simple image: her beloved reading beside her in bed, quiet, still, and so replete with her presence as to seem utterly indifferent to it. Without words they would nestle in a comfortable complicity. His eyes would be magnified by the glass of steel-rimmed spectacles, his book contained in an ecclesiastical handclasp of interlacing fingers and tilted, just so, to catch the angle of lamplight (from a lamp pink-coloured and tulip-shaped and chosen pragmatically not for reading after all but for the romantic tint of its radiance); his naked chest would rise and fall — in ever so mere and relaxed a fluctuation; and his face would be exquisitely close and illuminated so that every flaw, blotch and incipient wrinkle was clearly apparent, so that it was a face known and loved in its complete specificity.

Paulina looks out through the window pane at the backwards racing suburban scenery — the shadows are still stretching, the light almost sunless — and thinks this static vision supremely amorous. It combines in delicate balance expectation and satiation, is both ardent and exemplary.

The man reading *King Lear* has shifted in his seat, being somewhat hedged in by a woman of copious dimensions who perspires conspicuously and scowls at the world under a vestigial moustache. He has changed position slightly so that Paulina can see his face in an averted three-quarter profile and now notes once again its quality of captivated studiousness. The man has partly creased his brow as though the madness of Lear is beginning at last to perplex him, or as if, perhaps, he is haunted by some disturbing intuition or reminiscence inspired by speeches shouted in his head at the pitiless heavens. Paulina watches his face, summons, almost involuntarily, certain random though generically allied fragments of quotation (*Pour on, I will endure; This is the worst; I am bound on a wheel of fire; Blow winds, crack your cheeks. Rage, blow!*), and registers with care her second reflection.

It was years ago when, as a young undergraduate, she had gone alone to a campus viewing of a Russian movie of *King Lear.* In those days she was less shy and more self-dramatising, and clothed entirely in black and boldly singular, she had sat spectacularly in the very front row. What she saw was this: it was a black-and-white film, laboriously subtitled and epically miserable. There were Slavic faces streaked with rain and contorted in close-ups of unbearable anguish. Lear himself was bedraggled beyond endurance and had grief-veined eyes of watery translucence that seemed always to be at the point of brimming to tears. There was a Fool epileptic, a Cordelia ethereal, a Gloucester noble and a series of camera shots which, when not so close as to record each single blink and drawn breath, were taken from high in the sky, from a God's-eye-view. In a particular scene (she now recalls it), maddened horses fretted within their compound, whinnied and kicked and set the whole screen shaking — or so it then seemed — with the force of agitations occasioned by the tempest. And though lightning brightly and stereotypically flashed and thunder loudly and melodramatically boomed Paulina found it all entirely riveting. So much rain and suffering, the torsion of perspectives between the intimate and the planetary. By the end of the movie she felt herself storm-wracked and reduced to tatters and left the cinema, moved out into the night, and, unembarrassed by the stream of leaving students, simply burst into tears.

Could she have said what she cried for? Could she have known? The buildings are black and skidding silhouettes as the train shudders to another halt and the man reading *King Lear*, to Paulina's astonishment, lifts his migrant face and glances up for a second. He appears to meet her gaze, but it is instead one of those unfocused occasions of momentary distraction, for within the space of another second or two he is re-entrenched Shakespearian. It has been a moment of unseeing, of unintercepted isolation.

Paulina's third reflection — and this one seems to her the most difficult and involuted, the most in need of examination — is of a blinded child. When first she read *King Lear* it was not so much Lear's storm and madness that troubled her, but the motif of blindness. For as she read, in that state of cautious part-incomprehension that attends the young literature student, continual reference to the inefficiency and failure of eyes caused her mounting anxiety. At the point at which the Earl of Gloucester is threatened with blindness, Cornwell, his captor, utters words of awful cruelty: *Out, vile jelly. Where is thy luster now?* and this was to Paulina so dreadful a line — among many others, it must be said, that had conspired to place her in dread of what she was reading — that some fissure opened in time, and the lost memory of an event in her fifth year returned.

She had been living, in those days, with her impoverished family in a working-class country town, a time she recalls now as always governed by sensations of vague hunger and drowsy heat. Next door lived a fatherless family of numerous children, the youngest of whom, an infant of two, was left alone, tied in her cot, when her mother went out to work. Paulina visited this child from time to time, since the house was always left open and with her own siblings at school this was at least, in a five year old's practical estimation, a form of company. One day attracted by unprecedented screams, Paulina entered to find the child standing up in her cot with an eye gouged out and the other broken and damaged. Eye matter streamed down a face which seemed entirely fluid, composed of blood, tears and features which in their agony were robbed of distinctiveness. Paulina remembers thinking — in a childish and matter-of-fact comparison — that the ruined eye resembled shattered jelly. On the floor of the cot lay a bloodied fork which, along with various other household objects and appliances — a tin teapot, a spoon, plastic cups and a wire sieve — had been left, somewhat pathetically, as infant playthings. In a slightly delayed response Paulina was engulfed by revulsion. She fled to summon her mother and dully remembers that she spent the rest of the morning alone as her mother accompanied the child to hospital. That night — and how lucid and compelling this single moment is recollected — her father, presiding at the dinner table, waved magisterially his own fork in the air, nodded in the direction of the neighbour's house and pronounced in a tone of gravest accusation: 'It is that woman who is blind'.

The train has achieved a rhythmic motion and here, in the belly of this sliding machine, faced with this unnegotiable distance between that memory and herself, between the reader and her curiosity, Paulina suspects that her total repression of that event was not, as might be expected, some protective consequence of its gory spectacle, but rather of her father's words. As if physical ruination were not enough, he implied the existence of a realm of non-material wounding, of guilty negligence, of what in the gaudy and hyperbolic mode of childhood imagining represented an almost Shakespearian order of destruction and contamination.

The large woman sitting opposite heaves herself upwards to prepare for disembarkation. The train again slows and Paulina, now filled with a quality of sad estrangement, looks intently at the man's face as if in so doing she might will him to notice or acknowledge her presence. In a few seconds of stillness he remains inaccessible.

Outside the sky has blackened and in an optical, night-time trick of the light, her own face has appeared in apparition on the window. It hovers like a ghost in the dark, phantasmally vague, and now, with the train's increasing acceleration, appears lightly carried along, as though keeping steady pace or in ingenious concert.

With — what form of resolve is it, in fact? — Paulina decides at last that she will speak. She looks again at the man's face, at his snow-accustomed eyes, at the portentousness of his frown, at the lips, still parted as though such reading might require a little more oxygen than usual, at, last of all, the bowed curve of his nose, and unscrambles a sequence of potential words. She must not sound intrusive or rude, nor gauche or academic. She must not signal attraction, nor present herself as unfriendly. Yet as she hesitates and pauses, fixed with such purpose upon this man, this man reading *King Lear*, this man with whom, despite the strict quality of immurement which surrounds him, Paulina wishes to form some interrelation, she simply cannot heave her heart into her mouth. The train rocks and lurches and she actually says nothing. Nothing at all.

Paulina's destination is finally near. She and the insubstantial face on the window rise up and sidle into the corridor. The man continues to read, his eyes downcast. And as she steps out onto the platform she catches a last glimpse of him through the bright square window; bent in a kind of scholarly pose, the very picture of a man reading, like some clever and intricate Elizabethan engraving, he is also closed, unknown and now swept swiftly away, carried off noisily into the night.

Irrationally Paulina feels abandoned. With the other commuters she begins the walk up the railway platform and imagines, again irrationally, that perhaps her ghostly face is still riding on the window, watching the man reading and still trying to discern his exact location in the drama. The black sky stretches above, so saturated with her feelings as to appear entirely starless, and Paulina thinks of King Lear stumbling stupidly through the storm, of his jingly jangly Fool, so illogically wise, of this city through which she nightly travels, unconnected to anybody, isolated in a tissue of complicated memories; she thinks too of her beloved, tantalisingly distant and existing in visions, of the infant with no eyes, dissolving into tragedy, of cinematic tempests raging in black and white, of pinkish lamps, of the slow turning of pages, and finally, most peculiarly, of a few words in strange recurrence: 'learned-by-heart'.

The House of Breathing

From my grandmother Bridget I inherited a vision.

She told it so often and so variously, with such detail and so many embellishments, that it became more convincing to me than my own experiences and memories; we collaborated to affirm it, shared it indivisibly like impossible Siamese twins of two bodies but one heart. As a child I remember exclaiming: I see it! I see it! and she leaned forward, embraced me, encircled me with a scent of lavender and old-woman mustiness, and replied in a serious whisper, Why yes, I believe you do!

A ship. The Titanic. The sinkable Titanic. There it is sailing through darkness, slow and magisterial, with all lights ablazing. It is absolutely resplendent. There are rows of light-bulbs, festively numerous, and these everywhere illuminate decks and portholes, riggings and railings, and spill to spread nervous reflections on the surface of the ocean. It is as though the ship cannot contain the brilliance within it, but must whiten its surrounds like a purifying force.

And it proceeds, cumbrous and steady, sailing forward into a more dazzlingly white embrace, smack into its fatal icy rendezvous, smack into history. See it shudder, tilt and slowly submerge. It upends with a kind of sigh as though the sea opens a mouth. Tiny human beings fling themselves from it. Screams. Drownings. The gradual engulfment. Those lights in an eerie and wavering descent. The sea at last sealing lips over its watery secret and shock waves going sshh!, sshh!, sshh!

Bridget's particular Titanic — always stunningly well-lit and remarkable as much for its bright procession as its famous immensity — sailed, collided and sank in slow motion again and again throughout my childhood.

We lived in a desert-bound mining town, surrounded by thousands of sea-less kilometres of red dirt, stringy mulga, sharp spinifex and hard boulders (so dry, so hot, so finally unnautical), yet she transported her Titanic to our exact vicinity. It sailed past slag dumps and poppet heads, past the ore-crushing and extraction plants, down streets lined with Jacaranda, overflowing hotels and brothels that glowed like furnaces with their scarlet lights, and drifted real as ever into my bedroom each night. Its four enormous funnels. Its nine decks higher than buildings. Its eight hundred and eighty-two feet of ship-shaped and riveted steel.

And on occasions when my father was compelled to work night-shift — down there, getting gold, with his own lamp upon his head — she stayed perched on my bed for hours, rehearsing her monodrama. Her only story. Again and again. My room was almost floodlit with the power of her descriptions.

In April 1912 Bridget had been fifteen years old and a junior maid. (It was the thing, she said, to have a servant with an Irish accent; we were considered naturally servantish, our voices told them so.) Her mistress, Mrs Armstrong-Colman, was travelling to Boston to meet with her American relatives, and had decided on the White Star Line's new ship Titanic as the most salubrious passage. A woman of some means, she booked a first-class cabin for herself and her travelling companion Miss Thompson-Smythe, and for her two accompanying maids third-class berths.

As it happened Mary Riordan, the other and older servant, was taken ill in the week before embarkation, so only Bridget attended the women on their trans-Atlantic journey.

What I always remember first, she said again and again, is the dome on the top deck; it was like a giant glass bubble, stuck there between two funnels.

The women mounted the gangplank and entered the ship by way of the first-class staircase which was entirely covered over by a church-sized dome of glass and steel. As they descended beneath it Bridget glanced upwards and saw sunlight refracted through the faceted glass and thought it the most beautiful thing she had ever seen. An ornamentation entirely impractical. Constructed simply for effect. 'Utterly splendid', as Mrs Armstrong-Colman might say. Bridget looked down and saw the furenswathed backs of the women; they each clutched at the railing and followed a pert little man in white gloves and a neat hat. She paused, looked back up a second, brief time — it was so altogether captivating, so transfiguring of the sky, so deftly manipulative of light — and then scampered after them.

Often Bridget would inscribe her glass dome in the air for me. She raised her arms very high and swept her hands in broad gestures over the surface of an invisible hemisphere. Imagine a bubble, she said, only reinforced with steel. And then she added 'Utterly splendid!', using Mrs Armstrong-Colman's voice.

Bridget was dismissed at the door of her mistress's cabin — having been given a list of instructions and work duties, several reprimands in advance, and a reminder of the virtues and necessity of chastity.

She felt suddenly very girlish and not at all like a Maid-with-an-Income and a Position-with-a-Good-Family. She feared, now alone, both the magnitude of the ship and the lack of Mary's company. She feared, since third-class berths were lodged down in the very bowels of the vessel, just above the boiler and engine rooms, near the rumble and churn of the ship's metallic innards, down there, beneath the waterline, with no lamps upon heads if the lights should go out — she feared to sleep alone so very deep in the Titanic. The steps leading downwards seemed to go on forever; she now clung like an infant to the decorated iron railings and cursed Mary Riordan for her untimely illness. No pert little man in white gloves and hat led her way. No dome overarched. The whole area was shadowy, enclosed and suffused with the crude stench of machinery and new paint.

This was the reason, you see, I was on the deck when we hit the iceberg. Part of the forward deck was roped off for third-class passengers — that was our little area of freedom and fresh air — and I spent as much time out of the cabin as possible.

When Bridget was not required to attend the needs of the two hyphens (as she would later name them), she did not return to her cabin but wandered the territory of the stratified ship, climbing up and down its nine levels of iron staircase, creeping along corridors, peering through windows and portholes and doorways. As a maid she had a pretext for entering first-class areas: if she was challenged she simply responded that she sought her mistress, Mrs Armstrong-Colman, and excuse me sir, sorry sir, is she here then sir? She sought no permission, but simply exemplified the smiling effacement of maids and was often, in consequence, quite undetectable.

By this means of deliberate trespass Bridget gradually discovered the exorbitance of the ship: she saw swimming baths and squash courts, and the gymnasium within which jolted bizarre mechanical contraptions (a stationary bicycle, a flapping rowboat, an absurd model camel). There was a reception room where a band seemed perpetually to play waltzes. Dining rooms of darting waiters and obese millionaires. Smoking rooms — these specially impressed her — lined with potted palms and patterned mirrors and full of wealthy young men in decadent poses — legs crossed, heads thrown back, and arms draped in languid extension over the plush backs of armchairs.

And last, but not least, the Turkish Bath. When she glanced through the doorway at the entrance to the Turkish Bath she could not believe her eyes. It was decorated Sultan's-palace-style, with Persian rugs, brass lamps and masses of drifting fabric. Attendants wearing turbans and bright baggy pants carried fans made of peacock feathers which they lazily swung. Splashes and tinkling laughter could be heard from behind veils. And the whole room, lit in scarlet, seemed to glow like a furnace. It was thoroughly glamorous. Bejewelled. Incredible.

On the second night of the voyage Bridget discovered an area of upper deck allotted to third-class passengers and at last found a place in which she need not sneak or dissimulate. The deck was rather crowded; over it roamed a motley and often unseaworthy assortment of travellers, most of whom were emigrants to utopian America, dreaming wonderful dreams of skyscrapers and dollars. They chatted, smoked, and played at deck quoits and cards with unusual competitiveness.

In their company Bridget found herself less lonely and forsaken. She enjoyed the easy and rudimentary nature of their amusements, listened to their gossip, and sat late in the dark against the railing, feeling the sea air pass over her body, watching the pleated ocean stream backwards from the ship. A waltz could be heard, hanging quite magically in the icy night wind.

Not romance, but nearly, she often said; and I gave the word a capital R, presented the young man with a face a little like my father's, and for years vicariously mourned his tragic drowning, entrapped there, unsaved, his cry knocking against my heart.

As she was about to retire that second night Bridget met a young crew member who had escaped from the engine room to have a smoke. He was embarrassed to be caught; it was so late he assumed most of the passengers would be asleep. Yet as he spoke Bridget discovered that he shared her Irishness; he was from County Clare, from the very village, in fact, in which her own grandmother had been born; and Bridget was pleased that here, down here in third-class corridors, where the air stank of oil and machinery and reverberated with the rough, ore-crushing sound of reciprocating engines, that she could speak of her home and name her kin.

The two sat smoking together on the floor of the corridor with their legs outstretched across it, as if, after all, they both owned the place. And when he left to return to work he kissed her cheek, and she blushed, and put her hand to it, as though his lips had in some way marked or indented her.

A kiss, she said, just like this; and she would kiss my cheek, and I would blush and put my hand to touch, as though the young man himself, ardent even as a ghost, had inspired or inspirited it.

In between administering small services to the two rich hyphens, Bridget often climbed the stairs to visit the dome. She liked to see it at different times of the day, to watch how it glowed and changed, how it trained yellow beams to various sections of the staircase. This was how, much later, she always thought of first-class, governed and overhung by this fantastic jewel, this encompassing light. Then she would return to Mrs Armstrong-Colman's cabin, to brush her mistress's hair or lay out clothes, or prepare cups of tea from the wood and marble sideboard.

The cabin seemed to her sumptuous — its scrolled sofa, its cheval glass, its sideboards like catafalques — no more, of course, than in Mrs Armstrong-Colman's Warwickshire home, but remarkable because it was transferred to a ship. Bridget marvelled, unrevolutionary, at how certain people always carry their own worlds with them, reproduce materially their own importance, remain always defined by whatever surrounds them.

I was often lost. Sometimes I would panic when I came up or down a stairway and had no idea where I was, Grandma said.

And I, who had never been lost — my own town being flat and low, every street and house known to me — thought then of my father beneath the earth, hidden away in some tunnel, almost incarcerated. It frightened me to know nothing of the dimension he worked in. I was afraid he would one night disappear as my mother had. So finally. Forever.

It was something like an underground mine, with its confusing depths and levels, but also nothing like a mine; it was so strictly partitioned, its inner areas demarcated by style and admission. In her own cap and frilly apron Bridget was always climbing stairs and passing between the layers of different sorts of people; and though she usually seemed to know which section she was in, she often had to ask directions back to the third-class stairway.

She liked best to be up high, up there, in the light, where the great bulb of the glass dome was and where the names of millionaires circulated in the air like seagulls: Astor, Guggenheim, Straus; where she could linger at the fringes of the first-class dining room, observing fluttering serviettes and gorgeous women.

Secretly Bridget wished most to enter the realm of the Turkish Bath, but attendants would only let her peep for a second through the doorway. This prohibition was enticing. At night, in her cabin, way down there, she lay on her narrow bunk disrobing behind veils of gauzy fabric, feeling peacock fans fluctuate like wings over her body, and imagining herself clothed only in a scarlet light.

The collision. The collision.

That night was very cold and she was rugged up warmly. Stars were like sequins. A waltz flowed in the air. The wind from the north was freezing and continuous. And moving through the dangerous darkness and the contentious waves the Titanic shone so brightly that it coated the surface of the ocean with flecks of shimmering light.

By twelve-thirty most of the card players and chatterers had gone to bed, and there were only a few stragglers remaining, smoking or talking in hushed, private voices. Bridget had planned to wait for another hour before retiring — in the hope of encountering a second time her compatriot and his kiss. She sat against the ship's railing, breathing the fresh briny air. Inhalation, exhalation: the simple pleasure of night-time wind entering deep into the lungs.

The music now sounded deliciously Romantic. She thought of women with breasts and bracelets, of tiaras and champagne glasses, of long dresses, swirling.

It loomed out of the darkness like something unreal. More vitreous than the dome, uncannily pale, it seemed to proceed towards them, as though it, and not the ship, was driven and determinative. People on the deck began shouting with excitement and Bridget stood up very quickly, all the better to see the sight. Until the very last moment she thought the ship would veer or swerve to avoid the iceberg, but instead they moved slowly and steadily into conjunction, perversely waltzing, each fixed absolutely on its stubborn course. There was a jolt, a shudder, and the loud screeching sound of tearing metal. Broken ice fell heavily on the forward deck. Cries and exclamations. Mariners somewhere running and issuing orders. The band hesitated slightly in its musical rendition, then blithely continued.

In that strange period of suspension all on the deck were exhilarated. Under the hard starry sky they played football with pieces of ice and skidded to waltz music. Bridget laughed and clapped. She joined in the fun, kicking and sliding and feeling ice sting her hands with its extraordinary coldness. But then, remembering her duties, she left to seek out the two hyphens in order to tell and reassure them.

Because the music was playing I thought everyone was safe. It charmed us, that music. It was like a terrible trick.

From the lifeboat Bridget could see people gathering at one end of the ship as the other inclined and dipped into the water. She could see the bulging dome, and lights so radiant and supernumerous that they coated the ocean with silver scales. Music, waltz music, crept by her upon the waters. And because she was young and unknowing, because she was on an adventure, and dazzled, bewitched by spectacle and allayed by sweet music, she did not really believe that the Titanic would sink. As she listened to the melody and the soft plash of oars, she wondered again when she would meet her Irishman and his kiss. She touched her own cheek. She watched the ship recede. The darkness gather.

Only later did she learn of the fifteen hundred lost souls, of the crew, of the band, and the shortage of lifeboats, and of the multitudes in third-class who in the alarm and confusion, way down there, became lost. Forever.

When the ship was at last out of sight, a series of shock waves arrived. They made a noise like whispers: sshh!, sshh! Mrs Armstrong-Colman, who had managed to bring her mink, placed both her fur-covered arms around Bridget, encircled her with a powerful scent of lavender water and must, and wept.

* * *

It was nothing recondite or strange. I simply absorbed and enjoined with my grandmother's fixation, took upon myself her hysterical reminiscence. This gave my childhood and my home an odd imaginary quality: the broad streets of my town, with their civic buildings of desert sandstone, their large verandahed hotels and their low houses of wood and corrugated iron, were somehow less significant to me than the many-layered floating world Bridget repeatedly described. The shingly earth and the saltbush country, blazing in the sunshine, were dim by comparison with her light-bulbed ship and its golden dome. Shaft holes and mines, which other children regarded with casual disinterest, became indicative of depth and truly fearful. And there, in the desert, I grew obsessed with drowning.

At first I did not comprehend Bridget's story. I saw only a ship, glorious with lights, slipping below the ocean as my grandmother floated away. But then my mother died, so suddenly and unimaginably, and I became inquisitive and troubled by intimations of closure. I recall asking Bridget what became of the young-man-and-his-kiss, and she said simply that he drowned. Of course. He drowned. (Did I not understand that?) And it was only then, concentrated on the Irishman, that I registered for the first time a sense of consequentiality. I could see him washed in the darkness, fed on by strange fishes. His young face was like my father's, but sea-changed and vague, and his body dangled on the currents, lifeless and inert. A design of ripples slipped back and forth over his two workman's hands, so that he was no longer human in even that most human of places. Flux and reflux upheld and surrounded him; seaweed of many kinds wreathed and entangled him; he was cruciform; unfathomable.

With no vision at all of my mother's death, I saw — with awful clarity — this stranger's entirely.

Thus haunted I also became condemned to repetitions. In particular I developed a habit of listening to the waves of my own breathing: inhalation, exhalation; inhalation, exhalation. I would awaken in the middle of the night, in the middle of the scary, fluid darkness, and place my hand over my mouth, to check that I still lived. Inhalation, exhalation: I was bent on immortality. In addition — and with that propitiatory impulse of childish superstition — I secretly named my own bedroom 'the house of breathing', so that my safety was guaranteed, even as I slept. In contrast to the breathless rooms of the sunken Titanic, my room was breezy and undrowned. Life-preserved. Water-tight. Ventilated and air-conditioned. Buoyant, in the end, as any millionaire.

The desert wind, like a lover's emissary, flew directly through the window to kiss my cold cheeks.

As well as her obsessive retelling of her tale, my grandmother developed a lifelong practice of somnambulism. Every now and then she would rise up from her bed and roam the Titanic that existed in her head. Through shallow pools of moonlight and spilling shadows she mimed the climbing of stairways and gawking at the dome. She moved from third to second and first-class, into smoking rooms and gymnasiums, and sought out the young man or waited on the deck. She paused at the entrance to the Turkish Bath, precluded even in dreaming, and continued on, with dreamy slowness, through each and every spectral and memorised level. Aroused, I would awaken her, take her by the hand, and lead her back to her bedroom: it became a kind of ritual of all of our years together.

Sometimes, however, she seemed flushed and distressed, believing herself lost and trapped somewhere down in third-class; so I would guide her gently to my own bed and place her there to sleep beside me, keeping her very safe, utterly safe, in the house of breathing, where, despite everything, one remained alive during the night.

And if she began crying, which she occasionally did, I would put both my arms around her, encircle her completely, and whisper in my own voice sshh!, sshh!

BIBLIOGRAPHICAL ACKNOWLEDGEMENTS

The following books have been employed in the composition of these stories, either by citation or as reference.

1. MODERNITY
   Jurij Lotman, *The Semiotics of Cinema*, Ann Arbor, 1976.
2. THE ASTRONOMER TELLS OF HER LOVE
   A E Roy & D Clarke, *Astronomy: Structure of the Universe*, Adam Hilger, 1977.
3. OTHER PLACES
   Jill Jolliffe, *East Timor: Nationalism and Colonialism*, University of Queensland Press, 1978.
   Bill Nicol, *Timor: The Stillborn Nation*, Visa, 1978.
4. THE PRECISION OF ANGELS
   Fr Pascal Parente, *Beyond Space: A Book About The Angels*, Tan, 1973.
5. DARK TIMES
   Richard Holmes, *Shelley — The Pursuit*, Weidenfeld & Nicolson, 1974.
   Paul Foot, *Red Shelley*, Bookmarks, 1984.
   Thomas Hutchinson (ed.), *Shelley: Poetical Works*, Oxford University Press, 1970.
6. 'LIFE PROBABLY SAVED BY IMBECILE DWARF'
   Ronald W Clark, *Freud: The Man and the Cause*, Granada, 1982.
   Peter Gay, *Freud: A Life For Our Time*, Dent, 1988.
7. VERONICA
   Thomas Mann, *The Magic Mountain*, Penguin, 1975.
8. ON THE PITEOUS DEATH OF MARY WOLLSTONECRAFT
   Edna Nixon, *Mary Wollstonecraft: Her Life and Times*, J M Dent, 1971.
   Mary Wollstonecraft, *Vindication of The Rights of Woman*, ed. Miriam Kramnick, Pelican, 1975.
9. THESE EYES
   William Shakespeare, *King Lear*, Signet, 1963.